the thought of you

Neurospicy Book Club
Book One

allie lasky

For every neurodivergent person finding their footing.
It's okay. It's going to be okay.

one

. . .

Johanna

WHEN I GET the notice in the mail, I curl into a ball and cry. How the hell am I supposed to find a new place to live in thirty days when I can barely afford rent as it is?

There's a knock on my door and, wiping my tired eyes, I wrench it open to glare at the intruder.

It's Josh Sinclair. Of course it is.

"This a bad time?" he asks.

I forgot we were having dinner and a movie tonight.

"I'm fine," I tell him. "Come on in."

We've struck up a weird sort of friendship since graduation two years ago. We weren't close when we were in school, but four years of being part of the same athletic department, plus a year serving on the disciplinary council together, have made us… I don't know if we're friends. He texts me occasionally and we'll meet up for dinner or drinks or get together with his buddies from the gym. It's a good thing, I guess. Truthfully, I've become even more reclusive than I was in college. I barely leave my apartment except for work or to get food.

The studio is—tiny. There's my bed, a small sofa at the

foot of it, and a dresser that doubles as a TV stand. My itty-bitty kitchen has two counter stools, so I can theoretically have company over, but the only person who ever comes is Josh. He won't let this thing between us go. I don't know why.

"Do you want to talk about it, or do you want to ignore it?" he asks as he settles on my couch, opening the brown paper bag he brought with him. Chicken Alfredo, baked ziti, and spaghetti and meatballs with extra garlic knots. He pulls out a glass bottle of orange soda and a six-pack of beer.

"I can't stay here."

Josh blinks up at me, his green eyes owlish behind his thick, black, plastic-framed glasses. "Like…"

"My lease isn't being renewed."

"Shit. I'm sorry," he says. "If I hadn't just signed for a new place last month, I'd suggest we move in together, but…"

I shake my head. "It's fine. I'm fine."

He laughs, not believing me for a second. "Yeah, okay. Whatever."

"Where are you moving?"

Josh looks away. "Um…"

"Don't worry, I'm not trying to crash your living situation." I've never lived with a man before—aside from my father, of course—and I'm not about to do so now.

"Actually…" He chews his lip. "Did I tell you that Theo and I moved in together?"

I gape at him. "What?"

"Yeah. Me and Theo, we're living together…"

Jumping onto the couch, I swat at him. "That's huge!"

"Yeah, well…" His cheeks are red. "It's not like we weren't spending every night together already. Usually at my place, sometimes at his. It's just…"

His phone vibrates. He pulls it out and answers the call. "Hey, babe, I'm at Jo's," he says.

"Did you tell her?" comes the tinny voice of his boyfriend.

"I'm about to, chill," Josh says. "Can I call you back?"

"Sure. Love you," Theo says. "Tell Jo I love her, too."

Smiling tightly, I call back, "Love you, too."

My skin feels tight, like there's not enough elasticity in it to cover all my limbs and joints. I weave my hands together to crack my knuckles, and the satisfying crunch helps me acclimate, so I begin to methodically crack each and every joint.

"We're getting married," Josh blurts out.

I stare at him. "What?"

"Me and Theo. He—I know it's soon, but…"

My mouth is open, and I close it, very carefully debating my next words. Sometimes I say things before I think them through, and that's not something I want in this situation.

"Josh, I'm happy for you, I am," I tell him honestly. "It's just… you haven't been together long."

He shrugs. "When you know, you know."

It takes a few seconds for my brain to catch up with me. When the enormity of the situation hits me, I shove him. Because he's six-foot-seven and huge, the former volleyball player doesn't budge.

"Dude, you're getting *married*."

He picks at the peeling label of his beer. "I was kind of hoping you'd stand up with me."

My eyes pop open. "What?"

We barely know each other. We're only sort of friends. I tolerate him. He doesn't actually like me.

"You're…" Josh swallows, and for the first time, he looks nervous. "You're my best friend, Jo."

"I am?" My voice squeaks.

To my surprise, he nods. "The last two years… I'm really glad to have you in my life. And I want you to stand up with me and Theo and his brother as I celebrate the fact that I'm finally living the life I want to live."

"What about all your volleyball friends? Your cousins?"

"You know as well as I do that I don't talk to that crowd anymore." Josh shrugs again. "I don't want a big to-do. It'll be a small wedding."

I don't think his former teammates took his coming out very well. His parents certainly haven't. Just like me, his world has narrowed smaller and smaller in the last few years, and as more of our friends couple up and get married, there's that much less time to do things together.

Josh shakes his head. "I got distracted. Theo and I are moving in together and getting married. We just signed a lease. He lives with his brother in a two-bedroom across town, and he's looking for a roommate."

"I don't know…"

I've never lived with a man before. And I don't know that I want to live with a stranger, either. I did that for four years in college, and it wasn't exactly fun. I need my space to decompress. That's why I'm living in a shoebox of a studio apartment—it's all I can afford right now, but at least I can be alone.

"Just think about it," Josh says. "It's a decent apartment, the rent is dirt cheap, and it's right on the T, so you won't have to walk far in the winter."

"Why's it so cheap?"

"Their dad owns the place—they lived there when Theo was growing up. The rent covers the mortgage and bills, and since the mortgage is so old, it has a great interest rate." He shrugs. "It's a great apartment. We thought about moving in there together, but since his brother is in the second bedroom, we thought a fresh start might be better."

"But you want *me* to live with his brother?"

I've hung out with Theo half a dozen times in the year they've been dating, and we text and chat online regularly, but I've never been to his place or met his brother. There's never been a need.

Josh stares at me. "Well, you know him."

"I do?"

"Sully," he says.

I wrack my brain, trying to put a face to the name. "Who?"

"Sullivan, the football player? He went to Newton with us?"

The only guy I knew was a guy a year or two after me, a playboy douchebag who had a new girl on his arm every hour of the day.

"*He's* Theo's brother? Theo *Caldwell*?"

Sullivan is big and beefy, and Theo is… well, he's the definition of a twink. Slight, slender, and looks like one strong wind will blow him over. It's especially funny to see him beside his partner, considering there is over a foot difference in height between them and Josh is about three times as wide.

Josh shrugs. "Technically, they're step-brothers, but their parents got together when they were in kindergarten, so they're just family. They don't see the division."

"So you want me to live with *Sullivan*?"

We had a few classes together over the years, and yeah, we used the same dining hall in the athletic student center, but we didn't *know* each other. I doubt he could even pick me out of a lineup.

"He's not that bad," he says defensively.

"I don't know the guy!"

I can think of a handful of times we've spoken in the last five years. The only time we've ever had a protracted conversation was—

New Year's Eve.

On the roof.

I still don't know what to make of it.

In college, I didn't go to frat parties, but I heard enough about his reputation to know *exactly* what kind of guy he is. He was infamous in our small school for how often he got around.

And now I'm going to have to live with *that*?

"Just see the apartment," Josh urges. "You might change your mind."

"I won't."

two

. . .

Sullivan

I FOUND YOU A ROOMMATE, my brother texts me at three o'clock in the morning.

Great. Awesome. Rolling over, I shove my phone beneath my pillow and try to go back to sleep.

My phone vibrates again.

Aren't you going to ask who it is?

He's goading me. Taunting me. Like he has every day for the last nineteen years since our parents got married. Hell, even before then—his antagonizing me on the kindergarten playground is why our parents were called into the principal's office in the first place, where they met and fell in love.

But if Theo has had nineteen years to perfect his teasing, I've had an equal number of years' practice ignoring him.

As long as they pay their rent on time and don't leave dirty dishes in the sink, I don't really care; I text back, then pull my blankets up over my shoulders.

When my phone buzzes for a third time, I debate throwing it at the wall. But that will only leave me with more damage to clean up.

It's Johanna Chen, my brother tells me.

Instantly, I'm wide-awake.

Johanna Chen. She wants to live here? With *me*?

With a jab at my phone screen, I call Theo and his throaty laugh greets my ear.

"Go to hell." My voice is scratchy and hoarse. "You're fucking with me."

"Wish I was," my brother says. "Josh got her to agree."

"What, did he blackmail her or something?"

Not that she's probably ever done anything worthy of being blackmailed over. She's—

Okay, well, she's not the *nicest* person ever, but I honestly think she's just misunderstood. Nobody gets her the way I do.

Nobody *wants* to understand her the way I do.

As my mother, the psychology professor, explains it, I'm pretty much the poster child for neurotypicals. And Johanna? She makes all my spidey senses tingle in a way that I've never experienced before.

"Dude, you have problems," Theo says. "It only took Josh two weeks to get her to agree. You sure you want this?"

"Yeah, yeah, whatever. Mock me later. What the fuck did he say?"

Turning on the bedside light, I toss aside my covers and start pacing around my bedroom. Charlotte makes a clearly annoyed noise and hides her face under the covers.

Johanna Chen wants to move in with *me*.

"He says they'll come by and see the apartment tomorrow afternoon. Well, today, now."

"Yeah, fuck you very much for the three o'clock wake up call, by the way."

My brother laughs. "You're welcome. Don't tell me you're actually sleeping alone?"

"She left two hours ago. I'd just fallen asleep."

"Billy, one of these days you're going to get tired of your whoring around and—"

"First off, don't call me Billy," I snap. "And I'm not going to be able to anymore, am I? Not if she—"

I stop in my tracks.

Johanna Chen wants to *move in* with me.

"Why are you doing this to me?" My voice comes out as a croak. "What the fuck did I ever do to you to make you do this to me?"

"It'll be good, Billy," Theo says. "Now you can get her off your mind."

"Not gonna happen."

I've been trying desperately for the last five years, and I'm nowhere closer to being over her. We met at a freshman mixer for the athletic department, and while the attraction on my side was immediate... so was the disdain on her side. As soon as she found out I was on the football team, her walls went up.

We had a few classes together over the years—because she majored in Multimedia and Design, and it was my minor, there were a fair number of classes that overlapped. She thought I was a playboy football player (true) and only taking the classes to get an easy A (not true). From day one, she wrote me off as nothing, and I've been trying to get her out of my system ever since.

I sleep around. I've made no secret of that. I'm not in a relationship, I'm not dating any one person; I'm single, and that's the way it's going to be.

Because the only woman I've ever wanted anything more with wouldn't look at me twice.

And now... she wants to share a bedroom wall with me.

"Maybe now you'll get over this ridiculous crush you have on her," Theo says.

"Yeah, or maybe she'll crush me." That sounds more likely.

Although... I wouldn't say no to being crushed between her strong thighs.

"Just promise not to scare her off," my brother says. "You need someone to fill that bedroom, she needs a place to stay, and she doesn't need you going all crazy psycho stalker on her."

"I'm not a stalker. I just… appreciate."

Theo snorts. "That's something a stalker would say."

"I only admire from afar."

"Again, sounds like a stalker."

My bedside clock flashes at me. It's 3:14 AM.

"Fuck you," I tell my brother.

And then, like I should have a long time ago, I hang up on him.

It takes approximately half an hour to clean the living area of the apartment, and another forty minutes to tidy up the kitchen. Now that Theo and Josh are shacking up, my brother might be out of the house for three or four nights in a row, and I've been a little lax about my housekeeping without someone else in the apartment to check in on me.

There's a knock on the door, and I open it to find my brother, his fiancé, and—

I swallow.

"Hey." My voice comes out hoarse, and I clear my throat. "Come on in."

Theo and Josh exchange amused looks, but they step back to let Johanna pass ahead of them.

She's even more gorgeous than I remember.

Her posture is straight and stiff and her dark hair is in a slicked-back ponytail, the column of hair swishing behind her as she walks past me. I catch a whiff of her vanilla perfume in the air. She's dressed comfortably in jeans, a white t-shirt, and a lightweight jacket. If she's wearing makeup, I can't tell. Although… her cheeks are kind of pink.

"So, uh, this is the place," I tell her, waving my arm around the small living area.

Her dark eyes narrow as she evaluates the worn leather couch, the floral loveseat and matching armchair, and big-screen TV in front of a dingy coffee table. There's a round wooden table with four matching chairs separating the eating area, the vinyl plank flooring worn and cracked in places.

"It's not much," Theo jumps in.

She purses her lips. "Hm." She looks at him. "Can I see the room?"

My brother doesn't take the lead she's so obviously giving to him.

"It's just through here," I say, hooking my thumb towards the hallway.

The apartment is simple, but it's home. Our bedrooms are almost equal in size, plus or minus five square feet, and the shared bathroom is down the hall. There's a singular window overlooking the courtyard behind the building. The bedroom itself is painted a bland yellow color, and as much as I try to convince my dad to let me paint, he keeps putting me off.

Theo has only been out of here for a weekend, so I haven't had a chance to fill the room with all my shit. If she doesn't move in...

Well, it'll be tight financially, but it will be okay. I think.

Johanna looks around the room critically. There's a lamp in the corner that Theo left behind and a few empty hangers in the closet.

She looks at my brother again. "How much sage do I going to need to burn to cleanse all the dirty, dirty sex you two had in here?"

I choke. Josh goes beet red.

"Or maybe bleach," she continues, tapping her lips with her finger. "Hm. Maybe both."

Theo laughs, laid back and confident. "Definitely both."

My chest gets tight at her easy friendship with my brother. I had no idea they were friends until he posted a picture online of the three of them out to dinner six months ago. Since then, he's been taunting me daily about my "unrequited feelings."

I've made peace with my feelings long ago. She's not interested in me. Fine, whatever. I'll deal with it.

After a quick detour to the bathroom—she pronounces it satisfactory—and a peek through the kitchen cabinets, Johanna turns to me for the first time.

"How much is the rent?"

I name the number Theo paid—exactly equal to my own.

She nods. "I can do that."

"My parents own the apartment and the utility bills are all in their name," I continue. "Some months the bills will fluctuate with heating and electricity costs, but I'll give you as much notice as I can. I transfer them the money every month —you can give it to me or directly to them, whichever is easier."

"Hm." She presses her lips together, thinking.

"I won't rip you off. I'm not trying to—"

She waves her hand, dismissing me with a roll of her eyes. "Whatever."

Fuck. My dick reacts immediately to the lack of interest in her tone, and as all my blood rushes south, I feel my cheeks heat.

"So, um, when were you thinking of moving in?" I hope I sound casual and not like the overeager puppy I am, anxious for head pats.

Or, ahem, a different kind of touching... or maybe a different kind of head.

Theo clears his throat. "Charlotte," he says.

My eyes widen. "Oh. Yeah."

Johanna's head swivels to my brother. "Who's Charlotte?"

"You'll hardly notice her," Theo says. "She's quiet, she

keeps to herself. Sleeps most of the time. She stays in his room a lot."

"She's really sweet," Josh adds. "She's still a baby, but she has personality."

Johanna frowns. "You have a kid?"

My heart stops, and I choke. "What? No!"

"Charlotte is a baby who lives in your room," she says, her voice hovering on snide. I don't think she's purposefully trying to be insulting. Her pitch goes up and her eyes narrow when she questions things, and it makes people think she's being rude, but really I think she's trying to hide her own insecurities.

Exhaling, I shake out my hands. "Charlotte is my kitten," I tell her. "You're not allergic?"

She tilts her head. "You have a cat?"

I point to the cat tree in the corner, and the perch by the front window. The litter box is in the bathroom—I don't know how she missed it—and the food and water dishes are on a plastic placemat beside the dining table.

Theo smirks. "He's a cat dad."

Rolling my eyes, I flip him off, and when she frowns again, I immediately put my hand in my pocket.

Johanna lifts her chin. "I have to be out of my apartment in two weeks. When can I start bringing things over?"

I swallow. "Anytime. Today? Tomorrow? Whenever you want."

"Do I need to sign a lease?"

My eyes go to my brother, who steps forward. "Yeah, my dad will email you something. Just a basic lease, month to month, small security deposit to make his insurance company happy. He's not planning on selling the apartment anytime soon. Unless the market explodes like it did a few years back, he's keeping the place forever. And if he changes his mind, he'll give you as much warning as he can."

She's quiet for a moment, running a finger over her lips as

she thinks. I can see her eyes darting around the room as she processes.

Finally, Johanna turns to me. "I guess we're going to be roommates, then."

Oh, fuck me.

three

. . .

Johanna

IN WHAT FEELS like no time at all, my meager belongings are packed up. It's all the big stuff left now, like my bed and my couch. Theo gave me Sullivan's phone number, and I've been meaning to reach out about logistics… but I don't want to open that can of worms. I've been communicating with Josh and Theo about my plans, so I can only hope they relayed the message to my new roommate.

There's a knock on my door, and with a sigh, I crack my neck before opening the door. Let's get this over with.

Theo and Josh are on my doorstep, looking like their usual mismatched pair in workout gear. Theo is maybe five foot seven on a good day, and Josh is at least a foot taller and about three times as wide. They're holding hands, looking adorably in love, and my chest pangs. I want that. I've never had that.

Waving them in, I'm surprised to find Sullivan standing behind them. He's maybe two inches shorter than Josh, and his body is thick in a way that the lanky former volleyball player isn't. He's wearing gym shorts and a cut-off tee, his strong arms on display.

"Oh. I didn't realize…" I swallow. "I didn't know you were coming."

Sullivan snorts. "It's basically in my job description."

"Oh?" I lift my chin to hide my crippling lack of self-confidence.

"Yeah, former athlete, forever a moving buddy," Josh chimes in. "All I'm missing is the truck and then I'd be, like, required to help everyone move."

I'm confused.

Theo rides a motorcycle to work at the bank and Josh takes public transport to get to his gym. I don't think Sullivan has a car—not many people do in this part of town, mainly because there's no real place to park on a permanent basis. The apartment doesn't have designated parking, either.

"We spent our whole lives lifting heavy weights for fun," Sullivan tells me. His voice sounds gentle, almost calming. "Now, whenever any of our friends needs to move, we're practically obligated to help. It's basically leg day." His eyes rove over my boxes. "Definitely leg day."

I've packed as much as I can into suitcases, and I've thrown a few things into tote bags, but there are quite a few boxes.

Sullivan gives me a half smile. "Between the four of us, we should be able to get everything in one trip."

I still can't believe I'm doing this. I'm moving in with a guy I barely know.

"Does the bed come apart?" Sullivan asks me. He surveys the mattress and boxspring on top.

"I think so, it's IKEA. I got it when I moved in here."

He chews his cheek, thinking. "Let's get the bulky stuff down first, then if we have to take it apart, we'll have room to maneuver. And worst case, we make two trips."

Josh nods, going for the mattress. "You ready, man?"

Before I can so much as blink, the two of them have the queen-sized mattress hoisted and are on the way to the elevator. I want to make a "pivot!" joke, but most people don't really understand my sense of humor, so I stay silent.

Theo grins at me. "Well, come on, then. Our turn." He grabs a suitcase in each hand, wheeling them out the front door.

Alone in my apartment, I take a deep breath, and when the world doesn't feel like it's about to cave in around me, I pick up a box and follow.

There's a rented truck parked at the curb. Theo stands beside it, outright ogling his fiancé as Josh's arms flex and bulge from the strain of lifting the heavy mattress. At least, I think that's who he's ogling. It would be weird for him to ogle his brother.

Not that Sullivan isn't—

Well, he's always known he's good-looking. That's part of the reason he's so unattractive. The perfect asymmetry of his face, the snaggletooth incisor and scar bisecting his lip, soften what would otherwise be a face too pretty to be real. His nose is crooked, like it's been broken a few times—and after hearing all the rumors, yeah, it wouldn't surprise me if he's been in his share of fights over the years.

But Sullivan is just so freaking *pretty*. He's got sandy hair, like it can't decide if it wants to be blond or brown, and hazel eyes framed by thick, dark lashes. After years of playing football at the peak of conditions, his body has softened slightly, rounding out and mellowing. His muscle definition is still pretty high; as I watch him lift the mattress, I can see the lines of his shoulders and bicep flex, and…

Quickly, I drop the box on the curb and turn away, jogging back up the short stairs to my building, and then up the two flights to my apartment.

I can't do this. I thought I could, but I can't.

The elevator dings in the hall, and the three guys step out.

"Theo, help me with the box spring," I tell him.

He laughs outright. "I don't lift heavy things."

My eyes narrow at him. "Help me."

"Here, I've got it," Sullivan says, stepping forward. "Josh, you good to take apart the bed?"

My friend nods. "Shouldn't be a problem."

Hefting the boxspring—it's not heavy, just bulky—I start to walk, and Sullivan calls out.

"Hey, give me a sec," he says, giving me another one of those grins.

"I don't have all day," I snap. It's hot, and I'm already getting sweaty, I'm wearing the wrong shoes, and I—

To my surprise, he laughs. "I just need a moment to adjust my grip," he says easily. "We're going as fast as we can."

My back itches, like there's someone staring at me that I can't see. It's that peculiar feeling of being watched. My skin starts to prickle, and my stomach lurches. Turning, I check behind me—but there's nobody there.

"You good?" Sullivan asks. He quirks a brow.

Straightening my spine, I nod. "I'm fine."

I'm always fine.

———

It takes forever, but in the span of two hours, we've fully packed the rented truck, and three and a half hours after that, I have a mostly furnished bedroom again.

Sure, there are a lot of boxes. A *lot* of boxes.

But my bed is put together again, freshly made with clean sheets, and I have a dresser and a side table with the essentials unpacked. Since my sofa doesn't fit in my room, Sullivan agreed to let me keep it in the living room with the rest of the mismatched hand-me-down furniture. I don't think he minds my navy blue couch considering the floral print loveseat looks like it came from a grandmother's house in the 1980's.

It's only four o'clock, but I already want to go to sleep. Maybe for a week.

Theo disappears with the empty truck, returning an hour later with three pizzas, a case of beer, and a six-pack of the fancy orange soda I like.

The air is thick with tension. What happens now? Do we just… hang out? Me and Sullivan and Josh and Theo?

"C'mon, Jo," Josh says, waving me over to the table. "Let's have your first meal in your new house."

I'm not sure when he came up with the nickname. Both he and Theo use it more than my real name these days. It's weird. Why does he think we're on a nickname level? Even my parents don't call me by a nickname. They named me Johanna, so they call me Johanna, unless I was in trouble and they needed to use my full name, Johanna Marie.

Very rarely did that happen, though. I wasn't the getting into trouble kind of kid. More of the keep to myself and keep my head down kind of kid. If it wasn't for soccer, I'd never have made any friends.

Fuck. If it wasn't for soccer, I still wouldn't have any friends.

Sullivan kicks out the seat next to him, passing over a paper plate and a bottle of orange soda.

"I'm guessing this is yours," he says, inspecting a second bottle. "Do you have a problem with us drinking beer?"

Shaking my head, I reach for the first pizza box. "Nope. Just don't like it. I'm more of a tequila fan."

He whistles. "Okay."

Narrowing my eyes at him, I lift my chin. "What's that supposed to mean?"

"Nothing. Hey, I like tequila, too," he says. "It's just that usually, people like things a little more mellow than that."

I shrug. "I'm not mellow."

"No," he says with a grin, "I don't think you are."

A shiver runs up my spine. I don't know what that means. I can't tell if that's a good thing or not.

Subtext doesn't make sense to me. I can't figure out what

people are saying *underneath* their words. Body language doesn't always tell the whole story. Why are people so confusing?

Falling silent, I eat my pizza. Theo and Josh are going to a coworker's birthday party—they invite me along, but that's weird, I don't know any of Theo's coworkers at the bank, especially not the birthday person.

"What are you up to tonight?" I ask Sullivan.

It's a Saturday night in the city. I'm guessing he's going to go out and hit up a club or a bar, maybe bring a girl home.

My lips flatten. I don't like that idea.

But it's his apartment. I'm just renting a room.

"There's a hockey game at seven," he says with a shrug. "Probably just going to chill."

"You're not going out?"

I don't think I suppress my surprise quickly enough because he scowls and takes a long drink of his beer.

"I don't go out every night," Sullivan says tightly. "It's your first night here. I want to make sure you get settled in okay."

Oh.

That's… sweet.

"Thanks," I mutter, taking a third slice of pizza.

Sullivan and Josh have each taken down the better part of a large pizza, leaving the third for me and Theo to split. The smallest one of us has a big appetite, too.

My stomach twists uncomfortably. It's just hitting me that I'm sitting at a table with three men I hardly know, one of which I now live with. This is uncharted territory for me.

Okay. So I kind of know Josh. And Theo isn't a stranger.

So I guess it's just Sullivan. He's setting me on edge.

I live with Sullivan. I know nothing about him.

"What do you do?" I ask, interrupting their conversation about—I don't know what.

Sullivan blinks at me. "Like…"

"For work. What do you do?"

"I'm an analyst at a publishing house," he says.

I blink. "What?"

He laughs. "I run numbers and figure out if a book is selling, and how much we should push and promote it."

I'm confused. "But… you majored in art." We had so many art classes together. I definitely remember that.

Sullivan shakes his head. "I majored in economics. I minored in art because I like it."

"Not for the easy A?"

He scowls. "First of all, it wasn't easy. And second of all, fuck you."

I freeze.

Theo laughs. "Fuck off, asshole. She's not used to you."

Clearing my throat, I stand and pick up my empty paper plate. Dumping it into the trash, I enter my room and close the door behind me, sinking down against it until I'm on the floor, the solid wood holding me up.

Tears prick at my eyes. I thought I could do this. I thought it would be… different.

He's still the same callous jerk I thought he was.

There's a knock at my door.

I don't answer.

Another knock.

"Johanna?" Sullivan's voice is tentative.

Fuck. I've never heard him like that.

Like he's worried. Like he… cares.

"I'm sorry," he says quietly through the door. "I didn't mean…"

Wrenching open the door, I push aside his big, strong body. His arm brushes against mine as I move past, and he reaches for my arm, but I'm already at the threshold to the bathroom.

"Are we okay?" he asks.

"I'm taking a shower," I announce.

I catch his eyes on mine in the mirror. His face is twisted. He looks seriously torn up about this.

"Okay," he says quietly. "Just…"

Shaking my head, I close the door, and I wait until I hear his footsteps recede before I pull off my sweaty, sticky clothes.

The water pressure isn't bad. There are a few streams that are bent out of place, and a bit of hard water build-up on the shower head, but otherwise, the tub is fairly clean. I certainly have no complaints about his tidiness.

It's only after I duck my head under the water do I realize I left my shampoo and soap in my room. I hope he'll be okay if I use his. Just this once.

His body wash smells like fresh, crisp air and cedar. I'm surprised to see he has face wash in here, too. And there was sunscreen and skin care products on the counter, too.

Then again, I'm not surprised to find he takes care of his skin. From the little I've interacted with him, vanity fits right in.

The water runs cool, and with a sigh, I turn it off and reach for my towel.

Except—

I have no towel.

Fuck.

"Josh!" I yell through the door.

There are footsteps, and then a knock on the door.

"Johanna?"

It's Sullivan.

"Can you get Josh, please?" I ask through the door.

He's bought me tampons before in an emergency, and once I accidentally flashed him when I fell off a chair because he made me laugh so hard. Out of the three guys, I can probably trust him the most.

"What's up?" my new roommate asks.

"I just—I forgot my robe and my towel, and I—can you please have Josh get it?"

"I can grab it. Where is it?"

My face flames, even though nobody can see it.

"Please. Just—" I let out a shaky breath, shivering. "It's on the back of my door. I left it on the hook."

"Be right back," Sullivan says. His footsteps move away, then about thirty seconds later, I hear him return. He knocks on the door again. "Here you go."

Opening the door the smallest, tiniest crack, I shove my arm through, and he puts the soft towel and my terrycloth robe in my outstretched hand.

Withdrawing my hand, I slam the door closed, then lock it for extra measure.

"Shit. Johanna," Sullivan sighs. "I'm not going to—I'm not trying to sneak a peek."

Quickly, I dry myself off, then wrap my wet hair up in the towel and pull on my robe. The front gapes open and I tie the belt tight, making sure it stays closed.

When I open the door and poke my head out, I don't see anyone in the short hallway. Making a break for it, I scurry to my room, closing the door behind me.

How the hell am I supposed to do this?

four

· · ·

Sullivan

JOHANNA STAYS in her room for two and a half hours. Theo and Josh leave, and I take my own shower—with a towel at the ready, of course—and her door stays closed.

Fuck. Is this how it's going to be? Constantly walking on eggshells around each other?

She has to come out of her room *sometime*.

And when she does, I'll be ready.

Letting Charlotte out of my room, I settle on the couch with my sketchpad, a new beer, and the hockey game. She winds around my legs, her tail flicking my bad knee, before jumping beside me and settling in her favorite spot above my shoulder.

The hockey game starts, and even though I try to focus on the screen, more of my attention is diverted to the woman down the hall. This is not the way I wanted this to happen. The last thing I wanted was to upset her.

Maybe this was a bad idea.

Johanna's door creaks open, and I hear her footsteps as the bathroom door closes. A few moments later, the water runs, and I make my move before I can regret this.

With Charlotte on my shoulder, I take my place in the

short hallway between our rooms and the bathroom. The door cracks open, and Johanna pokes her head out.

When she sees me, she freezes.

"What are you doing?" she snaps.

I thrust a shot glass in her direction.

"Drink this," I tell her.

"What? Why?"

"It's tequila. Drink this, and let's talk."

Striding back to the living area, I slump onto the couch, where my own shot glass is waiting. Charlotte lets out a disgruntled noise as I accidentally crush her tail. With a muttered curse, I fix my positioning, her tail flicks the back of my head, and she rubs her cold little nose against my ear.

Finally, after what feels like an eternity, Johanna follows me to the sofa. She sits on her couch—we had to move Grandma Shirle's armchair into the corner, which is good, because hopefully now I can get rid of it entirely. I'm not complaining about the free furniture, but it's been in this apartment since my dad and Theo moved in twenty-two years ago, and it's… time.

"So you wanted to talk?" She glares at me, holding the shot glass like it's poison.

Lifting mine into the air, I sip it slowly, then bite into the lime wedge.

Johanna doesn't.

She downs the shot without the chaser, leaning forward to put the empty shot glass on the coffee table. I catch a hint of her cleavage and force myself to look away.

This is *not* the time.

"I think we need to clear the air," I start.

Her eyes narrow, and her chin lifts.

"I didn't mean to upset you. I wasn't—I didn't think. I'm sorry. It was never my intention to make you feel uncomfortable. That's the last thing I wanted to do."

"You didn't." Her voice sounds hollow.

I think I did.

I think she's pretending.

"Okay," I say instead of calling her on it. "I still want to apologize."

She rolls her eyes. "Whatever."

"You don't have to hide in your room. You are allowed free rein of the apartment. It's yours, too."

"How *generous* of you," she says, her voice snide.

Oh, so that's how she wants to play it?

"Yeah, it is," I tease. "I could force you to stay in your room and only let you out for meals, but I thought, well, sharing is caring."

To my surprise, she laughs. "Whatever." With a roll of her eyes, she stands and brushes off her hands.

"You can hang out here. If you want."

Fuck. Do I sound as desperate as I feel?

I won't be able to go to sleep tonight knowing she's upset with me. And I won't be able to rest comfortably in here if she thinks she has to hide away for however long she lives here.

Johanna returns to her room.

Yup, I screwed this up.

But less than two minutes later, she's back in the living room, this time holding a throw blanket and an e-reader. She settles onto her sofa and spreads the blanket over her legs before picking up her e-reader.

"What'cha reading?" I ask.

"A book."

I roll my eyes at her dry tone. "I had no idea."

A few moments pass, and then she says quietly, "It's a romance novel."

"Cool. Anyone I would have heard of?" I keep my eyes on the TV screen, which is currently on commercial break.

"I don't know. Do you know a lot of romance authors?"

I shrug. "A few."

Her stare burns into me. My dick immediately reacts, and I shift to hide my automatic response to her intensity.

"I work for a publishing house."

Johanna's eyes narrow. "I thought you worked in contracts."

"Yeah, and I work on contracts for authors."

She sighs, tipping her head back. "It's smut. Alien smut by Sybil Hedgewick."

"And you read this often?"

She scoffs.

"Seriously, I want to know," I tell her. "I want to get to know you. I realize this—us living together—is kind of unconventional, but if you're going to live here, maybe we can be…"

"Friends?" Her mouth twists in distaste.

My stomach sinks at the disgust on her face. "Yeah. Friends. Whatever."

She's quiet for a few minutes, and I almost think she's going to ignore me.

"I don't have a lot of friends," she says quietly, her eyes focused on her e-reader.

"Well, I do," I say, puffing up my chest.

She rolls her eyes.

"And that means I've had a lot of practice with it, *and* I'm good at sharing, so my friends are your friends now."

"Yeah, I'll believe that when I see it," she scoffs.

"You've met my brother, right? Annoying as fuck? Fuck, the whole reason our parents met is because he didn't want to share with me."

Theo was such a little twerp—that hasn't changed. But when I think about doing life with my brother, or life without him, I know which one I'd pick every time. Even when he's a shithead, even when he's a dick, I still love the guy. I'd do anything for him.

Just as I know he would for me.

"I don't know. I don't have any siblings," Johanna says.

"Cousins?"

She shrugs. "Two on my mom's side are about ten years older than me, and three on my dad's side who are in elementary school."

"That's hard."

"Eh. We moved every few years until my dad got tenure, then again before high school so I could get into the new charter school."

"My parents live in the same house they've had since they got married when I was seven. My mom and I were in an apartment in Southie for a few years before that, and we stayed with my grandmother for a year after I was born."

"Your dad?"

My chest gets tight. "My dad is Raymond Caldwell."

I have my mom's last name. At work, I go by Sullivan Caldwell. One of these days, I'll legally change it, but it's such a hassle. Maybe when I get married.

My full name is Ashley Sullivan, Junior, after the fucker who abandoned my mom. As if Ashley wasn't a terrible enough name growing up, being called by the same name as that asshole still pisses me off to this day. Just the thought of him makes my blood boil. At least she gave me her last name. They weren't married, and my grandfather insisted on his last name being carried down. I like that I get to keep a piece of my family close to me.

Everyone who knew me when I was small calls me Billy. It started out as Silly Billy, when I was a toddler, then morphed into just Billy. Everyone else calls me Sully or Sullivan, which is what I prefer to be known as. My mom's last name is Sullivan-Caldwell, keeping both the name under which she performed her decades of research and my dad's last name. I didn't want to pick a new first name. I'm happy with Sullivan.

Johanna looks up at me, confused. "But—"

"My dad adopted me when he married my mom, and he's the only dad I've ever known," I say firmly. "My sperm donor went to get diapers when I was three months old and never came back."

Her mouth drops open. "Sullivan—"

I shake my head. "I have a dad. I have a fucking phenomenal dad. And when the time comes, when I'm ready, I'm going to be a kick-ass father involved in my kids' lives. I will do everything in my power to know they are safe and loved."

My breaths are coming fast and sharp, and I feel like I've just sprinted fifty suicides in full practice gear again. Charlotte flicks her tail along my ear, and I reach up absentmindedly to give her pets and try to regulate my breathing.

To my surprise, Johanna doesn't seem put off by my intensity.

"You want kids?" she asks.

"Yeah. I do."

Not yet—and I definitely don't want any surprises—but when the time comes, I want the same awe-inspiring love that my parents have. That my brother has with Josh. That my friends have found with their partners.

I can be happy without a partner. I am very happily single. But when I have the opportunity to find someone to spend forever with… I won't let it pass me by.

"Huh." She turns back to her book.

"What?"

"I wouldn't have guessed that."

"Why not?" I demand.

She shrugs. "I don't know. Just didn't think you'd like that. Didn't think you'd ever want to settle down."

"You don't know shit about me," I tell her.

"Clearly." She rolls her eyes and flicks her finger at her e-reader, turning the page.

Her disinterest is actually refreshing. I'm not going to lie; I've had my fair share of jersey chasers and party girls over the years. I was a big fish football player in a small pond of the athletic department, and I wasn't shy—about anything.

I've slowed down a fair bit since graduation. Now that I don't have football dictating the rigid schedule which I had to comply with for so many years, things have changed. I like my job, but it's not my life. I like spending time with my brother, but he's not my only friend.

There's got to be more to life than drinking every weekend and burying myself in anyone who shows a modicum of interest. I just don't know what that is, yet.

Johanna sits on the couch with her e-reader as I watch the hockey game and sketch. My hand moves automatically, tracing the curves and lines that have interested me for so many years.

When the game ends, Johanna sighs, then stretches. "I'm off to bed."

"Have a good night," I tell her, turning off the TV.

Charlotte meows, and Johanna tilts her head as she squints at my cat.

"Did she just—"

"She says goodnight." I grin. "You'll get used to it."

Johanna tries to hide her smile, but I see the corner of her lips turning up as she turns away.

With a sigh, I sit up straight and stretch. My knee is twinging, and my lower back is tight. I'm going to have to foam roll before bed.

Charlotte flicks her tail against the back of my head.

"I know, I know," I tell her. "It'll be okay."

I glance down at my sketchpad, at the portrait of a woman sitting on a sofa, absorbed in her e-reader.

Heaving a sigh, I force myself to my feet. It'll be okay.

five

. . .

Johanna

SULLIVAN and I figure out a routine that works for us. He gets up early and is gone before I'm out of bed. After work, I hit the gym in the building's basement for a quick workout, and as I'm returning to the apartment, he's heading out in his own workout clothes. By the time he gets back, I've already finished showering and eating dinner, and then by the time he's done in the kitchen, I'm ready for a last glass of water before bed.

So basically—I know he's there, he knows I'm there, but we don't have to interact. It works great for me.

Saturday, I have brunch with "the girls." As I brush my hair and get ready, I scoff and roll my eyes. They aren't my friends, not really.

Diana Whitehall was on the soccer team with me, and after she set me up on a blind date with her best friend, we absolutely *hated* each other. It was not fun.

But it was clear to see that Barrett was in love with her, and she with him, even if she didn't realize it. Now, Diana and I are good; she's dating Barrett, and he and I are actually friends.

And Diana has made sure that we stay in touch. Her

friends live in the city, and they get together as a group for brunch or drinks or whatever.

I have to admit, it's not terrible having a group of people that I can hang out with. Aside from Josh, who's always busy with Theo…

Okay. So maybe they're my friends. *Maybe.*

We meet for brunch at a little bistro in the trendy part of Cambridge. Diana gives me a warm hug—I'm not sure why, I've never been the hugging type—and Sam Burke beams at me. Mason Prince and Deisy Cruz break off their conversation as I approach, and they both give me what seem like genuine smiles.

I've never been able to tell if people are being genuine or fake. Maybe it's because most of my smiles are usually fake.

"Where's Mackenzie?" I ask as I take the only empty seat.

Of the group of friends, she's the only one missing—the only remaining athlete, still attending Newton State College, where we all met. She's a senior this year and captain of the basketball team. She's also the one I have the most in common with. We're both readers, and we'll share books occasionally, though she prefers paperback and I prefer ebook.

"She's on her way back from her game in Virginia," Sam says of her future sister-in-law. Her engagement ring shines brightly on her hand, almost as bright as her massive smile.

"We haven't seen you in forever!" Diana squeezes my hand.

When she releases me, I pull my hand into my lap so she will stop touching me.

"It's been busy." Looking over the menu, I pick what I want to eat—even though I already looked up the menu online and decided before I came.

"How's the new apartment?" she pushes.

Sam tilts her head. "You have a new apartment?"

"Moved last weekend. It's fine." Unrolling my napkin, I

set it over my lap and carefully arrange my silverware on either side of my plate.

"We'll have to throw you a housewarming party!" Deisy says.

"That's okay. I'm not really a party person."

Diana grins. "Okay, but if you change your mind, we're happy to help."

I take her comment at face value. She's always happy to help. She's always *happy*.

"We'd have gotten the guys to help you," Mason adds.

"It was fine. Josh, Theo, and his brother helped."

It's easier to think of Sullivan as Theo's brother than as my roommate. It creates a boundary. He's the brother of my friend's fiancé, and just because we happen to be occupying the same apartment, it doesn't make us friends.

I don't know if I can be friends with a guy like Sullivan. He's the complete antithesis to everything I care about.

Although… he's not much like I expected. He hasn't gone out once this week. There are some more beer bottles in the recycling bin than there were last weekend—not an excessive amount, maybe one a night.

Most evenings, I find him on the couch watching sports with his cat on his freaking shoulder like a pirate with a parrot. He talks to her like she's a person, and he feeds her from his plate. His sketchbook is always in his hands, but he tilts the pages away before I can ever get a glimpse of his drawings.

He mentioned something about having a friend over today, but since I was going out, I don't mind. He has a social life. If I remember him right, he has a *very active* social life. I can hardly blame him for wanting some feminine company after sitting on the sofa like a monk all week.

If Mackenzie had joined us for lunch, I might have been able to convince her to go to the bookstore with me. Instead, I'll take myself and stay out of his way.

I'm good at doing things by myself.

I'm good at going places alone.

I don't like it, but I'm good at it.

"If you need any help unpacking, let me know," Mason says. "I love organizing closets."

"Thanks." I smile tightly at her. We don't know each other well—I hardly know any of them. Why am I here?

The other women talk around me as we order. Sam is recently engaged to Miles, Mason is engaged to Tucker, and Diana thinks Barrett is going to propose after she's done with grad school in May. Deisy is close to marrying Amir, too.

All of their partners were on the football team together, and the group has always been fairly tight-knit.

In college, I had friends. Teammates. And then they all went in different directions and I lost touch. To be honest, I didn't try all that hard to keep in touch, and neither did they. I don't know if that says more about me or them.

Sam and Miles's engagement party is coming up. For some reason, she's invited me to be part of her wedding party. I'm really not sure why. Aside from the year that we lived on different floors of the same massive apartment building, we never really spent any time together. Occasionally I'd go to the parties she'd throw, but we didn't exactly hang out. I barely know her fiancé. Miles is chill, down-to-earth. I think he likes that Mackenzie and I are friendly.

They're getting married in the fall. It's sure to be a beautiful wedding. There are nearly double the amount of bridesmaids as there are groomsmen, so there will be two women paired with each guy. Sam has a much broader friend network, whereas Miles keeps his quantity limited to focus on quality. I kind of like that.

"We should make a night out of it," Deisy suggests out of nowhere. "We can organize your cabinets and everything."

"With tequila," Diana adds with a grin.

"I don't know, I'll have to check with Sullivan," I say idly.

And then I realize my mistake.

Sam's eyes go wide. "You're seeing *Sullivan*?"

"No. We're living together."

"Hold up. You're *living with* Sullivan?" Deisy repeats.

Confused, I nod.

"I didn't think he was seeing anyone," Sam says cautiously.

"I didn't know you two were hooking up," Mason says. "For you guys to move in… wow. It must be serious."

"We're not hooking up." A chill runs up my spine. "I just live there."

"I thought—" Diana looks at me, tilting her head.

"We're roommates. I'm renting Theo's old room," I explain.

"So you're not…?" Sam makes a vulgar motion with her hands.

"No. We're not sleeping together. We just share an apartment."

"Oh. Okay, then," Sam says, leaning back in her seat. "That would be weird."

The hair on the back of my neck tingles. "It would be?"

"I can't imagine Sullivan settling down," she says, shaking her head. "I mean, maybe he will one day, but… I don't know. Sullivan? With a steady girlfriend? That would be crazy."

Would it, though?

I'm not volunteering for the job—I don't want to do that with anyone right now—but is it really that strange to believe the guy who wants a family would ever want to settle down into a relationship?

For the rest of the meal, I pick at my food. My appetite is gone, and I don't know why. I have this inexplicable need to defend him, but the conversation has already moved on, and it would be strange for me to speak up now. It's weird that I'm dwelling on this. Right?

After brunch, Diana proceeds to hug me again, and Sam

and Mason get in on the action, too. I'm too exhausted to head to the bookstore. Even though it's my happy place, right now, I just want to crash.

Being around people is hard sometimes. I have to be so much more when I'm with people—more polite, more sociable, more friendly, more… everything. And at the same time, I have to be less—less caustic, less honest, less myself.

It's a hard line to balance.

Trudging up the stairs to the apartment, my hand is on the doorknob when I remember Sullivan and his *guest*. Ugh. I don't want to listen to the two (or more) of them going to town for—how long will it take?

Then again, I've been gone for nearly four hours. Maybe it's over already.

The TV is on, I can hear a hockey game through the door. The coast should be clear.

It is not.

Sprawled on the couch are Sullivan and a host of guys, the partners of the women I've just had brunch with.

They look up when I walk in the door, and I see the confusion on their faces.

Miles, Tucker, Barrett, Wes, and Amir are confused, at least. Sullivan isn't.

"Hey," he says with a nod. "How was brunch? Want a drink? I think there's still some orange soda left."

"I'm good, thanks," I say. My voice wavers, and I clear my throat, finally remembering to close the door behind me and lock it.

"Johanna?" Barrett says, from my sofa. "What are you doing here?"

I burst into tears.

Why is everyone questioning me today? Why can't I just live my damn life?

Miles and Wes exchange a look, and Barrett curses under his breath.

"Ignore me," I say, waving my hand. "Pretend I'm not here."

Rushing from the room, I head to my bedroom and close the door, sinking against the strong wood paneling as I sob. I don't really know why I'm crying.

Except I'm *tired*.

I'm tired of having to put on this mask for everyone else. I'm tired of people second-guessing me and my decisions. I'm tired of having to *make* decisions. I'm tired from the mental and physical energy it takes to assimilate into a group of people that theoretically I have things in common with, but whenever I'm around them, I feel so isolated.

There's a tentative knock on my door.

"Johanna?" Sullivan's voice is quiet, hesitant. "Do you want to talk about it?"

I shake my head.

Then, realizing he can't see me, I squeeze my eyes shut and rub them with the heel of my hand. *I'm an idiot.*

"I'm fine."

He sighs. "Okay. But just so you know, if you're not fine, that's okay, too."

Exhaling slowly, I get to my feet and open the door.

Sullivan is leaning against the frame, his big body taking up most of the doorway. He's taller than me, taller than I remembered, and he's so wide, he blocks my view of the hallway.

Concern lines his face. His brow is furrowed, his eyes worried.

"Do you want to join us?" he asks quietly. "Or do you need some space?"

"I don't know," I admit.

His eyes search mine—what he's looking for, I don't know. There's this pull between us, this energy in the air. I don't know what to make of it.

Slowly, his hand lifts from the doorframe, and I turn to watch as he sets his heavy hand on my shoulder.

Heat spreads through me, and my breath catches.

My knees buckle.

"Fuck," he breathes.

And then he's moving, pulling me against his big, warm body. Sullivan's arms wrap around me, holding me securely. He smells good, like the soap that fills the shower, and his broad chest is hard beneath my cheek. His hand lands on my back, at the place where my neck meets my shoulder blades, and he puts a little pressure there.

"It's alright," he says quietly. "Do you want me to get Josh?"

Shaking my head, I bury my face in his chest. "No."

He exhales slowly, his breath ruffling the top of my hair.

"I don't like this." My voice comes out quiet.

Immediately, he releases me, and before I can think about it, I grab him and pull him back into me. He sighs, tightening his arms around me.

"I don't like feeling this way."

"What way?" His voice is equally as quiet. Almost soft.

Into the safety of his chest, I admit: "Like me."

six

. . .

Sullivan

SHIT. My heart just broke.

The pain in Johanna's voice nearly did me in.

But the words… *Fuck.*

Right then and there, I resolve to do everything I can to make her happy. Whatever it takes. I'll do it. I'll do anything to erase her pain.

I'll do anything for her.

There are footsteps behind me, and I turn to see Barrett approaching, concern on his face.

"Johanna?" he ventures quietly.

She pulls out of my arms, pressing the heels of her hands to her eyes. She doesn't go far—she leans against the door-frame, a mere whisper away from me.

"I'm fine," she tells him.

"Okay, you're fine," he says slowly. "What are you doing here?"

He looks between us, at the lack of space between us.

"She lives here," I answer for her, my eyes hard as I stare him down.

Barrett raises his eyebrows. "Since when have you two been…"

"What the fuck!" Johanna wrenches herself away from me. "Why does everyone keep asking that?"

In an instant, the weepy mess is gone, and in her place is a spitfire. Her dark eyes blaze with fury.

"We're not together, we're not fucking, we just live together. I have my own damn bedroom. It's not that big a deal!"

"What she said," I add. "We're roommates."

He looks between us again, clearly thinking of that hug.

Fuck.

I liked having her in my arms. As much as I'm upset about what forced her to seek comfort in me, I'm glad that I was there for her to do so. I'm glad she didn't go running for Josh again. Maybe she's starting to trust me.

There's a soft meow, and Charlotte winds her way between my feet. She nuzzles against my shin before moving to Johanna, wrapping her tail around my roommate's ankle.

She freezes.

"Charlotte's just saying hello," I say quietly. "She wants to check on you."

Johanna squats down, and I clear my throat, because this puts her head near my dick, and I do *not* want to be thinking about the implications of this positioning.

"Hi, kitty," she says, holding out her fingers for Charlotte to smell, and when the cat nuzzles her, she pets the top of her head. "I'm okay. I'll be okay."

"And if you're not, that's okay, too," I repeat softly.

Johanna looks up at me. Uncertainty is a haze on her face.

"We don't have to be one hundred percent all of the time. It's okay if sometimes our battery runs a little low, and some days, we just do the best we can."

She swallows. "I think I'm going to take a nap."

Do not offer to join her.

"Do you want to snuggle with Charlotte?" I offer.

"Thanks," she whispers.

She wraps her arms around my cat, lifting her into her arms and rising to her feet again. Charlotte rests her head on Johanna's shoulder, looking content. Traitor.

Then again, if I had the opportunity… yeah, I'd trade places with my cat, no doubts about that.

"Any time." My eyes pin hers. "Seriously."

Johanna bites her lip. "Okay."

I squeeze her shoulder one more time. "I'll just be in the other room if you need anything."

She nods, her eyes big and round. "Okay," she whispers again.

"Have a good nap."

I don't want to pull away. I don't want to leave her.

But I have to.

Johanna moves further inside her room, closing the door behind her, and I exhale slowly.

"So," Barrett says quietly. "How long have you had feelings for her?"

"I don't know what you're talking about." My response is stiff and wooden, my eyes still on her door.

He snorts. "Please."

Is it really that obvious?

Rolling my eyes at myself, I push past him and rejoin my friends in the living room. The game is still on intermission, so I haven't missed much.

And, it seems, neither have the guys.

Miles and Amir wear smirks, Wes has his eyebrows raised, and Tucker is outright grinning.

"Okay, boys," Barrett announces as he flops back onto the couch. "We've got work to do."

"What kind of work?" I grab another beer from the fridge without offering them any, then rejoin them and take my spot.

"We've got wooing to do," Miles says.

"Excuse me?"

Wes rolls his eyes. "Anyone can see it."

"See what?' I ask.

"You're head over heels for that girl," Amir said, nodding towards the hallway.

Well, fuck. I'm not about to lie and deny it. Faced with the question, I have to be honest.

Taking a long pull of my beer, I exhale. "Yeah."

Miles and Barrett exchange a look.

"For how long?" Tucker asks.

With a snort, I shake my head. "You don't want to know."

"Dude, I pined over Mason for three years after our break-up. I know pining when I see it." Tucker rolls his eyes. "That one pined for Diana for years. Like, eight years." He nods to Barrett. "And Wes…"

"Longer than I should have," he admits, his eyes flicking to his girlfriend's brother. Mackenzie was almost nineteen when they got together, but they'd been friends for several years, even though he never considered making a move while she was still in high school. With their age gap, though…

I sigh. "We met at freshman orientation," I admit. "I asked her out, she turned me down, and that was it."

"Damn," Miles says, shaking his head.

"Pay up." Amir nods to him, and with a laugh, Miles pulls out his wallet and hands over a $20 bill.

"What the fuck." I glare at them.

Amir laughs. "Come on. Every time we were in the same room as her, you would stare at her."

"No, I didn't."

"Uh, yeah, you did," he corrects me. "I just didn't know if you wanted to fuck her or strangle her."

"Why not both?" Wes asks. "As long as she consents…"

Miles chokes.

"Well, fuck." I look at him, suddenly seeing him in a new light.

I knew Amir was into the freaky stuff, but I didn't think Wes would be.

Then again, considering how much he reads… yeah, maybe it shouldn't have been a surprise.

And hey… Johanna reads, too. Maybe she's…

My blood rushes south, but I know better than to adjust myself in front of the guys, because they'll just make fun of me for it.

I clear my throat. "So… what now?"

"Well…" Barrett cracks his knuckles. "Do you want to keep pining for the rest of your life, or do you want to make a move?"

"Definitely the first one," I say confidently.

Miles snorts. "You sure about that?"

"We live together. She's my roommate," I remind him. "It wouldn't be… I don't want to make her uncomfortable. It's awkward."

"I went on a date with Johanna once," Barrett says out of nowhere.

I glare at him. "No, you didn't."

"It was a blind date. A million years ago." He waves it away. "I don't think she goes out a lot. We barely see her anymore. She's withdrawn into herself since college."

He does have a point. Every single night this week, she goes to the gym in the basement and comes straight back to the apartment, and then goes to sleep early.

"Coax her out of her shell," Miles suggests. "Take her out without letting her know you're dating her."

"Just be her friend," Tucker adds. "If something happens, great. If not… well, you can continue to pine."

Glaring, I punch his arm, and he laughs.

"It could be worse," he says. "She could still hate you *and* want to move out."

My blood runs cold. Fuck.

seven

. . .

Johanna

SULLIVAN IS BEING WEIRD.

I don't like it.

When I emerge from my room after my nap, it's to find the apartment empty and the shower running. Charlotte follows me into the main living area and then jumps onto her spot on the couch, right where Sullivan usually sits.

He's tidied up after his guests—the bottles and cans are in the recycling bin, the trash has been taken out, and I think he's even mopped the floors.

A bottle of orange soda is on the counter, next to a full-sized Hershey bar and a neon yellow post-it with a happy face on it. Suppressing a laugh, I put the bottle back in the fridge. I like orange soda, I do, but I don't need it all the time. It's more of a special occasion treat than an everyday thing.

The Cookies 'n' Creme chocolate bar? Yeah, that's what I want right now.

There's a long, low groan from the other room, and I whirl in the direction of the noise. The water is running in the bathroom, the pipes humming.

Sullivan is—

There's another sound, almost like a grunt. Tilting my

head, I approach the little hallway that leads to the bathroom. The sounds are louder here. I can still hear the water running, but whatever he's doing, he sounds like he's in pain, or maybe...

Oh.

Sullivan is—*oh*.

The image of his big body springs to my mind. The hot, soapy water sluicing down his muscles... My body clenches, and the physical reaction takes me by surprise. What am I doing?

In my head, I imagine him wrapping that big hand around a dick that's probably equally proportionate, working himself over and over again.

And then I imagine I'm in there with him, his body pressed to mine, his cock in my hand and his mouth on my neck, sucking at that sensitive spot on the hinge of my jaw that always makes me weak.

It's been a while—a *long* while—since I've had the company of another person in my bed. There have been a few people since graduation, but aside from three dates with a coworker's cousin that ended in "It's not you, it's me," nothing has lasted beyond one night only. I'm not good at dating. I'm not good at *people-ing*, really.

In college, it was one thing to go to a party and find a cute guy to take me home. It was a small school, with an even smaller social scene, and I didn't have to venture far. Now... the city is big, and there are all sorts of strangers, and I don't know who I can trust to actually make sure I'm safe and having a good time.

And the bars Josh and Theo usually take me to are gay bars, so, well, I don't often find guys wanting to sleep with me there.

Through the bathroom door, I hear a loud, long groan, then a sound that—*did he just come?* The water slaps against the inside of the tub, a different pitch now.

My body flushes. I'm sweating, my face burning hot.

What did I just do? Did I seriously stand there listening to my (very hot, very attractive, very single) roommate masturbate?

It's possible that's not what he was doing. He could have had a tough workout, or be in pain, or—

Or he could have been touching himself, a voice says inside my head. *He's been trapped inside the apartment all week. He has needs. And you're not meeting them.*

It's not my place to meet his "needs." That's not what our relationship includes. Our *roommate* relationship, I stress to myself, is just two people who live in the same apartment in different bedrooms. Just because we happen to share a bath-room doesn't mean we're sharing a toothbrush. That's disgusting.

Just because he's jerking off in the shower doesn't mean—

The water turns off with a squeal of the pipes, and I rush into my room, closing the door behind me. Diving under the covers, I bury my face in my blankets. My heart is pounding, my blood rushing dully in my ears. I feel like I've just kicked the winning goal in a tough playoff game, out of breath and out of control.

Practice your breathing. It sounds like the child psychologist my parents sent me to when I was eight years old. I didn't like going—play therapy doesn't make sense, even to me now, and after a good six months of no improvement, they said I didn't have to go anymore.

I'm not sure why they decided I needed therapy back then, and I don't know if they even remember it. It's a hazy memory. Every other Tuesday I would go see the psycholo-gist, and then I'd get chicken nuggets from the drive-thru for dinner. Those were good days.

Rolling onto my back, I take a deep inhalation, count to four, then slowly exhale for four counts.

Again.

Inhale for four beats, pause for four beats, and exhale for four beats.

I've done yoga and pilates, which both incorporate breath work, and I've been working on my cardio fitness levels for the better part of fifteen years. But I haven't been this... flustered.

I wonder what he was thinking about.

Or who.

I just know it wasn't me. How could he? He probably doesn't even recognize that I'm female and "eligible". He hasn't made any sexual comments since I've been here. We co-exist in the common spaces, and that's it.

There's a light knock on my door.

"Johanna?" His voice is husky and hoarse. "I'm going to run out and grab dinner. Do you want to come with me?"

My brain gets stuck on those last three words.

Come with me.

Not, like, *go* with him to dinner.

But *come*, like I imagine he just did.

Shoving away my blankets, I approach the door and open it a crack.

Sullivan is standing in the hall, a soft green towel wrapped around his midsection. His body is—whew. I've been around athletes forever, and I've seen guys without their shirts on.

But Sullivan?

He was a safety in college, a few inches over six feet and maybe two hundred and ten pounds of solid muscle and strength. In the almost two years since he's graduated, he's softened some, but the muscles in his torso are still in stark relief. His pale chest is covered with coarse, dark hair, with a trail leading down to the knot in his towel.

A rivulet of water slides down his belly, and I watch it run with a fervent fascination. I wish I could follow it with my tongue. My nipples bead into tight buds, and a surge of wetness slicks my core.

His eyes are wide, and it takes me a second to realize that I'm wearing a white camisole tank top and a pair of panties. I took off my bra and my jeans when I got home for my nap, and I hadn't put them back on yet.

"Dinner?" His voice cracks. His eyes snap up to mine.

"Sure. What are you in the mood for?" I lean against the doorframe, chewing the inside of my cheek. *DO NOT CHECK HIM OUT. Do not make him uncomfortable.*

Sullivan swallows. "Um…"

"I was thinking of stopping by the bookstore, too," I add. "Do you want me to meet you after?"

He shakes his head, water droplets flying from his short hair. "We'll go together," he decides.

Together. I like the sound of that.

"I'll let you get dressed." My eyes cascade down his torso again. He clutches the towel around his waist, his biceps bulging and his forearms flexing as he tightens his grip.

"Sounds good," he says hoarsely. He licks his lips. "I'll let you know when I'm ready for you."

My eyes go wide, and I sputter out a cough. Does he—did he intend for that to sound—

"I'll be ready," I manage with a squeak.

When I emerge from my room twenty minutes later, I'm wearing both a bra and pants, and I duck into the bathroom to brush my teeth and refresh my makeup. I'm *not* dolling myself up for him, I'm not, I promise myself as I rub away the smudged eyeliner in the bags under my eyes and tie my hair back into a fresh braid. This is just… normal getting ready things. I would do this if I were going out with Barrett and Diana, or Josh and Theo, or anyone else.

This is most certainly not a *date.*

eight

. . .

Sullivan

THIS IS MOST CERTAINLY *NOT* a date.

Oh, and I'm in hell.

Johanna Chen moved into my apartment last week, and already, I want to die.

I didn't know she had tattoos, though. I'd caught a glimpse of one, a few years ago, and chalked it up to being KT tape on her shoulder blade. No—she has a half-sleeve on one arm, full color, and the outlines of another series on her left shoulder.

And that's ignoring the fact that she was wearing a see-through white tank top with nothing underneath, and a pair of bright blue boy-short underwear that I want to peel off of her with my teeth.

Despite coming in the shower a few minutes ago, I'm itchy and unsatisfied. There's a restlessness in my blood that makes me wish I were still playing football so I'd have the excuse to tackle someone and get my frustration out.

I'd love to tackle her and…

When the guys suggested taking her out, I thought it would be easy. Go grab a burger, maybe a beer, and just chill like we do here at home.

I didn't anticipate the fire in my gut at the idea of being seen out in public with the hottest girl I've ever met. I didn't know I'd feel like the luckiest guy in the world because *she* wants to go out with *me*.

Except she doesn't want to *go out* with me. We're just grabbing dinner. Chill, casual, roommate dinner.

Not like I'd be able to lay her in my bed and eat her out until she's had seconds, thirds, and maybe fourths, too.

I'm waiting in the living room when she emerges from her room, wearing a plain white t-shirt, dark jeans, gray suede boots that come up to her knees, and a black leather motorcycle jacket. It's not what she was wearing to brunch this morning—she'd put on different jeans and a ruffled blouse, though I think I do remember her carrying the same jacket. Her hair is pulled back into a loose braid, and already a strand is falling out of the style. I want to tuck it back behind her ear.

That's weird. That would be weird to do with a roommate, right?

"You look great," I tell her automatically, and she rolls her eyes. "I'm not just saying that. You look—" I exhale. My hands are shaky, so I tuck them into my jacket pockets. "You ready to go?"

She nods, slinging her small backpack purse over her shoulder. "You're sure you're okay going to the bookstore with me?"

"Yeah. It'll be nice, get me out of the house a bit." Patting my pockets—wallet, cell phone, keys, emergency condoms—I open the front door and usher her ahead of me, locking it behind us.

"You don't go out nearly as much as I expected you to," she says as we hit the stairs.

I stare at her back. I can't tell if that was a compliment or judgment.

"I really don't go out much." I most definitely am *not*

staring at her ass in those tight jeans. "I mean, my best friend lived with me. I didn't have to go far to hang out with him."

Reaching the bottom of the stairs, she turns to look up to me.

"Theo is your best friend?"

I nod. "He's my brother."

"And now he's across town," she says slowly.

"Yeah. We'll grab a drink after work this week, but it's not the same as coming home to him every night—or even every few nights, with him and Josh staying at his place so often before they officially moved in."

We fall into step beside each other. The bookstore is about three and a half blocks away, and the early spring evening is warm enough that I don't need to zip my jacket.

"I'm sorry I'm not him," Johanna says.

"I would never ask you to be."

"Still. He's your best friend."

I shrug. "His living with his fiancé isn't going to change that. He's found his happy ever after."

She hums. "Maybe."

Her lack of optimism doesn't bother me, though.

When I first met her, I thought she was cold, aloof. When I asked her out, she turned me down almost before I got the words out.

But the more I observed her make friends and settle into college life, I realized she's just shy. Some people are shy and soft; Johanna is shy and hard. Because she acts confident, is absolutely gorgeous, and doesn't tolerate any bullshit, it's easy to interpret her social awkwardness as being rude, but really—

I think she's afraid.

We reach the bookstore, and I open the door for her. She offers me a half-smile as she makes a beeline for the romance section.

Hiding my own smile, I follow her, ready to carry all of

her books. I can bench press 225 pounds for thirty reps; I can carry a few measly books.

When she lifts two thick tomes into the crook of her arm, I wordlessly offer my hand.

Johanna turns to stare at me. "What?"

I hold out my hand again.

Confused, she slaps my palm with hers in a low five.

With a laugh, I reach for the books in her arms. "I'll take those."

Her eyes narrow. "What are you doing?"

"I'll carry them, so you can find more."

She scoffs and rolls her eyes, which makes me smile. She's so adorable when she's frustrated with me.

"No ulterior motives. I don't mind."

"I'm sure you don't," she mutters.

But she hands over her books, and as I glance over the back covers, she plucks a third from the shelf, surveys the blurb on the back, then waves it in my direction.

"Dance, monkey," she says blandly. "Earn your keep."

I can't help it; I laugh. I laugh so uproariously, people start to look at us, but I don't care.

Yeah, this might not be a date, but that doesn't matter. I get to spend time with her. *That* is what's important.

There's a woman in the next aisle wearing a purple apron, stocking shelves. While Johanna is occupied, I approach her.

"Hi, excuse me," I say, and the worker turns to face me.

She's pretty in that generically pretty way, wavy brown hair and green eyes, with a stud in her nose. Her name tag reads SADIE. That's a pretty name.

She can't hold a candle to Johanna, though, not by a long shot.

"I was wondering if you have a book club," I ask quietly.

Frowning, she nods slowly.

"Specifically a book club that reads romance novels."

Now, her gaze narrows. "This isn't a place to pick up women. You can't—"

I shake my head. "See that woman over there? Leather jacket, tall boots, scowl like she'd kill a man with his face between her thighs, and not in the good way?"

Sadie purses her lips, following my gaze to Johanna, who is blissfully unaware of these goings-on.

"She could use a book club."

She hesitates.

"I swear, I'm just trying to help her out. She'd never ask herself," I add. "She's just…"

Sadie sighs. She pulls a business card out of her apron, writing something on the back. "We meet the second Thursday of every month in the back of the shop. BYOB."

"Awesome, thanks." I give her a winning smile, and she laughs and shakes her head, returning to her work.

Whistling, I rejoin Johanna, who has four more books in her arms.

Without a word, I pluck them from her hold, looking over them curiously. She was reading alien smut the other night, she said. One of the books is about dragons, two more are about a BDSM club, and one is a bright pink romantic comedy.

"What do you like to read?" I ask, flipping through the pink title.

"Books," Johanna says dully.

I laugh. "No shit. All romance?"

She shrugs, not looking at me. "Primarily."

"Paranormal?"

"Sometimes."

"Why?"

"Why what?"

"Why romance?"

"Because I like it," she says flatly.

"I know. But why do you like it?"

I don't really know why I'm pushing this. I want to know, yeah, but more than that, I want her to *tell* me. I want her to open up.

"Why do you watch porn?" she asks me.

I clear my throat, giving her a hard look, even as my dick reacts at that word on her lips. I adjust the pile of books in my arms.

"So that's all it is to you? A means to get off?"

She sighs. "No. I like the story. I like the fantasy. Some guy coming in and sweeping me off my feet. He wouldn't care that I'm..."

"That you're what?"

Johanna turns away, tucking a strand of hair behind her ear.

"That I'm me."

Stunned, I'm rooted to the spot as she turns the corner and approaches the next row.

When my brain kicks into gear, I scurry after her. "What do you mean?"

She looks over her shoulder at me, her forehead wrinkled. "What do I mean what?"

"That you're you? What does that even mean?"

She scoffs and rolls her eyes, but she steps closer and puts another book in my arms.

"I'm not the kind of girl that guys go for," she says. Her voice is flat, unemotional, and her eyes are hard as she glares at me. "I'm not cute or frilly or soft or sunshine-y. I don't like crowds, I don't get along with people, and I don't understand the joke. It's fine, I'm fine, I'm used to it. But I'm not going to pretend like I'm suddenly going to change." She puts another book on my pile. "I'm done."

"Done?"

"I've hit my limit," she says, waving her hand dismissively. "Come on, let's check out."

Chewing on her words, I follow her to the register, gently

tipping the pile onto the counter. Sadie, the employee I talked to earlier, checks us out as she checks us out. She organizes the books into two paper bags, and I take them right away with a murmured thanks.

"So did you get her number?" Johanna asks as we exit the store.

I stop in my tracks. "What?"

"You were chatting her up. Did you get her number?"

"Would that bother you?" I venture carefully.

PLEASE SAY YES. Please have an issue with me asking out other women. Please tell me that I should only be paying attention to you.

"You don't have to pretend to be interested in going to the bookstore. I can do things by myself," she says, rolling her eyes.

"I did get her number, actually," I say, and she scoffs. "The store hosts a romance book club. I thought maybe you'd be interested."

Johanna stops in her tracks. "What?"

"I mean, I can go with you if you don't want to go alone," I offer quickly, and she frowns. "I just thought…"

She crosses her arms over her chest. "That I have no friends and no life?"

I step closer to her. "You know that's not what I think."

Slowly, like I would approach a skittish kitten, I touch her shoulder like I did earlier today.

She takes a deep, shuddering breath, her body practically vibrating.

"I think you can do anything you set your mind to. But I also think you're so comfortable with who you are, you don't want to venture out and try new things. You don't let people get close enough to see the real you."

She bites her lip. Her eyes are fixed on mine, welling with tears.

"I think you're awesome, Johanna. I really do." I hope my

voice conveys my sincerity. "You deserve to be happy with who you are."

She swallows. "I really don't like you," she says, her voice shaky.

Recoiling, I remove my hand from her body immediately and take a step backwards.

That sound? That's my heart shattering into a million pieces. I feel like I've been stabbed in the carotid with a shard of glass pulled straight from my chest, and all of my emotions are leaking out onto the pavement.

Johanna gulps. "No, I mean—" She blows out a breath. "How are you so good at calling me on my shit? You don't even know me."

My heart races. "I know you better than you think."

She steps towards me, then pauses. "I didn't mean it," she says.

"Mean what?" I can hardly breathe.

"It's not that I don't like you," she says. My heart can't take this constant battering. "It was—that's my way of saying, you see me, and I don't know what to do about it."

"Is that a bad thing?" I ask.

"That you see me, or that I don't know what to do?" She looks lost.

"Yes. Both."

Johanna sighs. "I don't know."

"We don't have to figure it out right away," I say, and when she doesn't comment on the "we" I used, I consider it a win. "Let's grab dinner while we're out. There's a great Serbian restaurant down the street. Have you had Serbian food before?"

She falls into step beside me. "I don't think I even know where Serbia is on the map."

nine

Johanna

SULLIVAN'S BODY heat is like a furnace beside me. I angle closer to him. There's a chill in the air that wasn't present on our trip here an hour ago.

"I'll show you," he says with a half-smile. "It's in the Balkans."

"I didn't think you were so into geography."

His half-smile turns into a full smile. "My grandmother's family is from Serbia. She was first generation, so I'm third—my great-grandparents moved here right before my grandmother was born."

"Does your family live nearby?"

He shakes his head. "My grandparents passed a few years back, and my aunt is in New Jersey. My mom's in the suburbs—she teaches at Newton."

"Huh."

"What?"

I shake my head. "I knew you were originally from here, but I didn't realize you were *from* here."

Sullivan shrugs. "My old elementary school is three blocks south of our place. When my parents got married, they moved across town, and they moved me and Theo to a new school nearby."

"What does your mom teach?"

"Psychology." He gives me a sidelong glance. "It's because of her that I was accepted into Newton, and then I walked onto the football team, and that was it."

I stop.

"What?" He turns to face me.

"You walked on?" I repeat. That means he was good—maybe not good enough to get recruited, but he showed up on campus and demanded they pay attention to him—and then they *did*. He was a three year starting varsity player.

Guarded, he nods.

"I didn't know you could do that."

He lifts his shoulder. "I mean, I played growing up on the varsity team all four years of high school. I just didn't bother with the recruitment thing, because I knew Theo and I were going to Newton on employee family grants no matter what."

"Do you regret it?"

"No," he says immediately, and my eyebrows rise at the emphatic response. "No," he repeats, a little softer. "I don't regret it at all."

There's an intensity in his eyes that I don't understand. He's staring at me, his chest rising quickly, and a flush creeps up his neck and over his cheeks. What's got him so worked up? Why is he acting like this?

"C'mon," Sullivan says, nudging me with his elbow. "Let's grab dinner."

The restaurant is down the block, and as he opens the door for me, I'm struck by how effortless his chivalry is. He isn't being condescending. He doesn't go out of his way to brag about being a decent human being; he just is one. It's like the bare minimum of expectations, but I like it. He's always watching out for me, trying to take care of me.

I just wish he didn't have to.

Inside, he greets the hostess with a flirty smile, but his hand hovers over the small of my back as he guides me to a small table for two near the window.

I wish I could get a read on him. I don't think he's trying to get me to sleep with him. That would be dumb.

Even if it might be fun, I know hooking up with my roommate is *not* a good idea. Seen the movie, read the romance novel(s). He's hot, don't get me wrong, but if I know anything about Sullivan, it's that he sleeps around.

There's nothing wrong with that as long as it's all safe and consensual. And it seems like it is. But I know better than to hope to "change" a guy—especially someone like me, trying to change someone like him.

Fuck that.

I want to curl up into a ball and hide with my new books, but he's holding them hostage under his side of the table.

"What's good here?" I ask, picking up the menu. Everything seems to be... meat. Or cabbage. There are grainy photos next to the dishes. I place the laminated card back on my plate. "Order for me. Pick something I'd like."

Sullivan smiles at me, his eyes soft. "Okay."

When the waitress comes back over, he orders a variety of food, the unfamiliar words rolling off his tongue like they were his first language.

Which they might have been. I'm proficient enough in Taiwanese Mandarin, even though I mostly learned in school and not much at home. My parents mainly speak in Mandarin when they're trying to talk *around* me, so I won't understand, and even though I've taken seven years of classes and I'm able to mostly carry a conversation, I can barely write and I have a third-grade reading level.

"Are you fluent in Serbian?" I ask him.

To my surprise, Sullivan grins. "No. I can order off a

menu, I know household commands like clean my room and set the table, and I know all the curse words, but my mom didn't use it much growing up. She always says—"

He stops.

"What?"

He swallows, and his eyes lift to mine. "She always says she wants to teach it to her grandchildren."

"And that's... something you want?" My throat is dry, and I reach for my water glass at the same time he reaches for his, and my knuckles brush against his. A spark of condensation from his glass coats my fingers, the sensation oddly intimate.

"I do, yeah," Sullivan says steadily. "When the time is right, I want a family."

"But until then... what, you'll just hang out and sleep around with any girl who looks twice at you?"

He scowls. "Slut-shaming isn't very nice, Johanna."

Something about the way he says my name makes me sit up straight and pay attention.

There's a tension in his face that makes me pause. He's usually so easy-going. Lackadaisical, almost. I never thought of him as a human being with feelings. He's just... He's Sullivan.

Except he's not the guy I knew in college. That guy was objectively a tool, and he wasn't shy about showing off the woman on his arm for the night.

This guy? He's... he cares.

And it's clear that he cares about me. Why he does, I'm not sure, because all I've done is brush him off. But he's consistently been checking to make sure I'm okay, to offer comfort, to rescue me from myself.

"I wasn't."

"You were," he returns steadily. "I'm not ashamed of my past. I've slept with plenty of women, but they all knew going into it that it would only be physical. It would never be real."

My stomach churns at the intensity on his face.

"Why not?"

Sullivan exhales heavily, his eyes locked on mine.

"Because when the woman you're in love with won't give you a second glance, you find any way possible to cope through each miserable, exhausting day."

My heart skitters to a stop.

Sullivan—in love with someone?

Why does that make chills run down my spine?

His eyes are sad, his gaze locked on mine. My heart is breaking at the agony on his face.

"She doesn't deserve you," I tell him firmly. "Not if she's treating you this way."

To my surprise, he smiles. "Well, she doesn't know."

My breath catches. "You haven't told her?"

"She's made it clear," Sullivan says. He shakes his head. "Besides, I'm the one that doesn't deserve her."

"But you're sleeping with other women."

"I have slept with other women. I'm not currently," he explains.

That's news to me.

"Like…"

He shakes his head. "I was given a chance recently, an opportunity, and I'm not about to waste it. If she came to me today and said, let's get married, I'd do it tonight. I'd go along with pretty much anything she suggests."

My stomach churns. He has feelings—real feelings. It's clear this woman isn't some passing fancy for him. Whatever happened in his past, he's willing to put it all aside and change his entire life for a chance with his dream girl.

It's a good thing nothing could ever happen here. I'm emotionally unavailable enough as it is; I don't need to go after a guy who is obviously in love with someone else.

Again.

Unease prickles at the back of my neck, and I tuck a strand

of hair behind my ear to cover the urge to crawl under the table and hide.

I give him a hard glare. "So then, why are you here with me?"

ten

· · ·

Sullivan

I STARE AT HER.

Does she really not get it?

I didn't think I was being that subtle.

"Johanna…" I reach for her hand, only to be interrupted by the waitress setting down a plate of food between us.

Where the fuck did she come from? She wasn't here a second ago.

My roommate shrugs, running her thumb over the tines of her fork. "So, what is everything?"

I point out the dishes to her, traditional meat pastries, a cabbage and beef dish, roasted carrots, and an egg, cheese, and pastry pie that reminds me of home.

Not because my mother ever made it. No—my mom is a *terrible* cook.

My parents would order food from the little Serbian deli in our neighborhood, and we'd seek out these little pockets of our culture hidden amongst the patchwork of the city. There's a little bakery up in Medford that we'd get birthday cakes from, and a Czech pie shop in Dorchester where we'd go for savory pies, and a few other little places that other people seem to glance over.

Gamely, Johanna takes a little bit of everything, trying it all. As prickly as she is, she's not picky.

We're quiet through our meal. She's thinking heavy thoughts, if the furrow between her brows is any indication. And even though I'm hungry, I'm queasy at the thought of how close I came to telling her everything.

I want to woo her. I want to date her.

But I don't want to make her uncomfortable.

And while the guys may have dismissed it, I'm very aware that she and I are living together. We've managed a week of peace.

I just want a lifetime more of it.

When the check comes, I take out my wallet before she can reach for her purse, offering the waitress my debit card.

"We could split it," Johanna suggests.

"We're not going to split it," I tell her.

She frowns.

"You'll get the next one."

She sits back in her seat, looking me over shrewdly. "The next one?"

"What, you're suddenly going to move out?"

She blinks, confused. "No?"

"Then yeah, we'll grab dinner again sometime."

To my surprise, she doesn't seem happy about that. A muscle clenches in her jaw, and she looks down at her empty plate.

After a moment, she whispers, "Okay," tucking some of her hair behind her ear.

With a sigh, I shake my head. "You're not getting rid of me that easily, babe."

Her eyes blaze, and her mouth drops open, and I think she's finally, finally going to give me a piece of her mind.

But after a moment, she closes her mouth, swallows, and looks away.

"What just happened?" Leaning towards her, I gesture to her face. "What did you just do?"

She looks confused. "I don't… know?"

"You're hiding. Why are you masking with me?"

Johanna blinks. "I'm not wearing a mask?"

"Not literally. I mean—"

I blow out a breath. Does she really not know? Has she never put together this particular puzzle?

Maybe I only see it because of my mom's psychobabble in the back of my brain. I'm as neurotypical as they come, but when your parent spends thirty years studying neurodivergence in people assigned female at birth…

I notice. I see things.

"Masking is when certain people… hide away parts of themselves. The pieces that make them who they are. They pretend to be different so they can assimilate, and they lock away the parts that make them unique and special."

"I'm not doing that," she says instantly.

"Okay." I'll give her the benefit of the doubt. "But when you say that nobody would like the real you, and you don't like who you are inside… when you cut yourself off in the middle of a conversation, or when you think they don't like what you're about to say so you change the subject? That's considered masking, too."

"That's not me. I'm not," Johanna insists. Her eyes are hard, glaring again.

"Either way," I say, pushing forward. "I'm a safe place. You can be yourself with me. You can share those parts of yourself with me."

I don't know what's going on with the usually confident and composed Johanna. She's cracking. But I do like that she feels comfortable enough to expose those little fissures to me. It might not be on purpose—I don't think she's actually in control of her emotions today—but she could have clammed up and walked away.

She didn't, though.

"Are you okay?" I ask her seriously.

Her chin lifts, and her eyes narrow at me. "I'm fine." Her voice is snide.

But that's her mask. That's how she acts when she pretends everything is okay.

"You just don't seem like yourself lately." I keep my voice casual. "I'm here if you want to talk about it. About anything, really."

"How kind of you," she snipes.

With a scoff, she stands and pulls her coat off the back of her chair, shrugging into the leather jacket.

"I'm fine," she says again. "Oh, and Sullivan?"

She leans close to me, her mouth near my ear. The heady scent of her perfume nearly blinds me with lust, the same way it does every morning when I step into the bathroom and smell her soap lingering in the air. My dick starts to react automatically, and I inhale deeply, trying to memorize this moment.

"Fuck you."

She swipes the bookstore bags from under the table and stalks out.

———

I could lie and say I went straight home to confront her.

But I didn't.

Once she walked out... I needed some space. And I think she might have, too.

That's the problem with being in love with your grumpy roommate. You can't go home to get away from them. You can only hide.

And I don't want to hide from her. I do need to regroup and strategize, though. As much as I'd like to call up my friends and head to the nearest sports bar, I know that's probably a no-go after they all got away from their partners at the same time earlier today. And I know I don't want the entire group of happy couples telling me all the ways I screwed up the best thing in my life.

So even though it's been a long fucking day—seriously, it's been go-go-go since the guys came over this morning—I hit the nearest T station and make my way across town.

My brother lives in a fancy building downtown, near his job and close to where his fiancé works. The doorman eyes me curiously, but since my name is on the list, he lets me past the guard gate and I take the elevator up to the eleventh floor.

Theo answers the door shirtless, a scowl on his face.

"The fuck do you want?" he demands. "We're a little tied up at the moment."

"I need help."

"And I need to get laid," he snaps back.

"Wait. Like…"

"Yeah. *Tied up*," he repeats. "Can this wait?"

I debate. I really don't want to bother him. I don't want to interrupt his plans more than I already have, and if Josh is hooked up in some contraption, I don't want to think about their letdown at crashing their evening.

"I think I screwed up," I admit. "I can't go home right now, and my other thought was to go to a bar, so I came here instead."

He glares at me. "Well, come in then, asshole."

I clear my throat. "Do you want me to wait out here while you two finish?"

With a sigh, Theo scrubs a hand over his face. "We were just getting started."

I wince. "Sorry, dude."

Inside the apartment, he disappears into the guest room, rather than the bedroom they share. I hear the low murmur of voices, a needy whine, and then silence.

Okay, maybe I do need a drink, after all. I now know

enough about my brother and Josh's proclivities that I might need some brain bleach.

The case of Bud Light in the fridge makes me think of her. *She doesn't like beer.*

The bottle of tequila on the bar cart makes me think of her. *She prefers tequila.*

The vanilla scented hand lotion in the bathroom makes me think of her. *It smells like her.*

Everything reminds me of her. I don't fucking like it.

Theo joins me in the living room after a few minutes, pulling on a t-shirt. Josh is behind him, the six-foot-seven giant glaring at me. His face is flushed, his shirt doing a poor job at hiding the leather harness he's wearing beneath his clothes.

"We were busy," Josh snaps.

"I need help," I admit quietly.

He sighs. "Okay. What did you do?"

Theo goes to the fridge and grabs three beers. I take the offered can but don't open it.

"I don't think she's okay."

Josh rolls his eyes. "Probably not, if you're here."

"No. I mean—in the broad spectrum of things, I don't think she's okay right now. I think she's teetering on the edge of something, and I think the crash is going to be painful."

"What do you mean?" Theo asks.

Tugging at my bottom lip, I sigh. "She's cried in front of me more times today than I've ever seen her cry before."

"You didn't exactly know her before," my brother points out.

"Okay. Fine. Whatever. But she's also said she doesn't like herself, she doesn't have any friends, and she thinks people don't like her. I don't want her to be consumed by self-hate."

"You can't control someone's inner thoughts," he says.

Josh is pensive. "She's been melting down a lot lately. The Jo I knew three months ago is not the Jo she is today."

I shrug helplessly. "She's struggling, and I hate that, and I don't know what to do about it."

"Okay, but what happened *tonight*?" My brother glares at me. "You could have called."

"We went to dinner."

His eyes go wide. "You asked her out?"

I shake my head. "She went to brunch, and I had some guys over to watch the hockey game. She came home and immediately burst into tears, then locked herself away in her room. When I checked on her, she had a… not a meltdown, but something not great was definitely going through her head."

I pause, thinking over the day.

"I suggested we go to dinner to get out of the house, and she wanted to go to the bookstore, so we stopped there. And then she accused me of getting the sales clerk's number—which I *did*," I readily admit, "because the bookstore has a book club that I think would be good for her. And when I told her that, she had another little meltdown."

"Yeah, but how did you screw this up?" Theo says. "Other than, you know, being you?"

"We were eating, and everything was fine, and then she started masking, and I told her she didn't have to mask. And she said she wasn't." I run my hand through my hair. "I called her on her shit. She didn't like that."

Josh winces. "No, I'm guessing she didn't."

"I think…" I swallow, and crack open the beer. "I think she doesn't know."

"About your feelings for her? She doesn't, she's as blind as a bat," her best friend says.

"No. About her being neurodivergent."

Josh sits back, processing.

Theo hums. "You're probably right," he says after a long pause.

"She's struggling, she's having a hard time with life, and

maybe dealing with burnout on top of just being overstimu-lated all the time." I count each issue on my fingers. "She's living in a new place, surrounded by new people, and she just —she doesn't know how to cope. Her strategies aren't working."

"And how are you going to help her?" Josh asks.

"That's what I need help with. Do I tell her? I'm not a psychologist. I can't diagnose her. I just know because…"

"Because Mom," my brother says.

"Right. And if she's struggling with autistic burnout, the last thing I want to do is overwhelm her by introducing her to *my mother*."

"Hey, I like your mom," Josh protests.

"Oh, she's great," Theo agrees. "But she doesn't know when to turn off the doctor in psychology and when to be a normal person."

"Yeah." I bring the beer to my lips, then pull it away without taking a drink. "I just… I want to help her. But I don't want to push her away even more. I don't want her to resent me. I don't want to offend her."

"Or you could give her some much-needed answers to a question she doesn't know needs to be asked." Theo sighs. "There's no right or wrong way to do this."

"There's nothing wrong with being on the spectrum," I say emphatically.

My brother arches an eyebrow. "The language has changed. That's not the best way to say it. Just like high-func-tioning, that's an outdated label for a very real, current diag-nosis that people are finding later in their lives."

"You're right. I know better." I rub my forehead. "I should do better. And I don't want to send her into a spiral. I wouldn't love her any less if she—"

Josh raises his eyebrows. "If she…"

"She needs help," Theo says quietly. "It's okay to help her."

"It doesn't blur the lines too much? Roommate, friend, boyfriend, person that upended her entire life?" This time, I do take a drink of the beer. It doesn't chase away the anxiety sitting on my chest like an anvil.

"Okay, one, you're not her boyfriend," Theo says, and I scowl at him.

"Yeah, no shit."

"You don't have to be her caregiver. She can survive on her own."

Survive, but maybe not thrive.

"I don't want to be her caretaker. I want to *take care* of her. I just don't want her to…"

"To glom onto you, and use you as a crutch instead of finding herself," my brother finishes.

"Yeah. I want her to be able to stand on her own two feet, regardless of what's going on between us." I sigh. "And as much as I don't want to make a move on the person living with me, I want her comfortable in her own home more than I want to be with her."

"You're putting her needs before your own. That's all you've ever done," Theo says. "But Billy, it's okay to put your own oxygen mask on first."

I shake my head. "Not the right analogy. I'm not in crisis. I'm not on the verge of a breakdown."

"Except you're sitting here on my couch, interrupting my plans, when you have a fantastic girl at your place, and you're—"

"I don't want to mess it up more." I rub my forehead. "I just want—I want her to be happy, even if that means we can't be together. Even if it means turning her world upside down."

Theo sighs heavily. "Dude, I think you know what you have to do."

"Run away to Australia?"

My brother laughs. "No, shithead. Go get your girl."

It takes me another half hour to peel myself off the sofa, and another forty-five minutes to make the journey home. I can do this. I can do hard things.

When I get back to the apartment, though, Johanna is asleep on the couch.

On my couch.

Charlotte is wrapped up alongside her, and my cat meows quietly at me but doesn't move. Usually she's all about the head scratches. Tonight, she seems content to stay at Johanna's side.

I understand that completely, and in a weird way, I'm jealous of my cat for being able to receive the affection that I so desperately want.

It feels like crossing a boundary to carry Johanna to her room. And I don't want to wake her up—she looks so peaceful, finally at rest. Her e-reader is on the floor beside her, and I rescue it to the coffee table.

Grabbing one of my spare blankets from the linen closet, I tuck it in around her and press a light kiss to her forehead.

"Goodnight," I tell her, even though she can't hear me. "Sleep well."

eleven

. . .

Johanna

I'M WARM.

That's weird. Why wouldn't I be warm?

The scent of cedar surrounds me, lulling me into complacency like a soft lullaby. I don't know how smells can be like songs, but this one reminds me of home.

Not my parents' house where I grew up.

Not the dorm rooms I lived in during college.

Not the apartment I just moved out of.

It's a state of being more than a place. It's comfort, and familiarity, and warmth, and light, and... *home*.

There's a soft vibration near my ribcage, and as I wiggle myself into consciousness, I realize I'm on the couch. The noise is Charlotte purring, and the heavy weight near my hip is the cat's body. Her little face is tucked right up against my ribs, her whiskers tickling my elbow.

As I shift, she lets out a sigh of displeasure.

"Sorry," I whisper to the cat.

I don't recognize the blanket on top of me. Sullivan must have—

Sullivan.

What did Sullivan do?

Or rather, what did I do to Sullivan?

Ugh. My head falls back against the side of the couch, and I scrub a hand over my face. My watch says it's about four o'clock in the morning. I have no idea when I fell asleep. The last thing I remember was reading my tablet, and now it's on the coffee table beside me. It certainly isn't where I left it.

Last night—it's like I was naked. He's able to see through me so clearly. I don't know how. I don't know why. I just know that I felt so exposed, sitting in the restaurant at the little table with him, and it wasn't a good feeling. He calls me on my bullshit. He knows I'm a fake, a fraud. He knows I'm nobody.

The blanket is soft, a well-worn fleece that's the right weight of heavy and smells like cedar and the detergent he keeps in the laundry closet.

Charlotte nudges my elbow with her nose. I give her a few pets as I recalibrate.

Do I pretend like it didn't happen? Do I just avoid him forever and move out next week?

I can't do that. I can't afford to move again, and I can't afford rent at another apartment, and I can't—

I can't.

With a sigh, I sit up and swing my legs over the couch. Charlotte jumps down to the floor with feather-light feet and darts away. I fold the blanket and set it on the end of the sofa.

What do I do now?

Making my way back to my bedroom, I pause at the threshold, then return to the sofa and wrap the blanket around me like a cocoon.

It smells like Sullivan. I don't know why that's so comforting, but it is.

Pulling back my own covers, I slide into my bed, keeping Sullivan's blanket wrapped around me underneath my regular sheets and blankets. It feels like a hug. Aside from yesterday afternoon, I can't remember the last time I had a hug—a real hug—and not just a perfunctory greeting. I'm not a touchy-feely type person, but I do appreciate a little bit of physical affection, and it's been a long time since I've been in a position to let myself experience it.

Before long, I fall back asleep, and when I wake up, the sun shines through my window. With a yawn and a stretch, I catch sight of the heavy green fleece blanket wrapped around my torso, and a smile comes to my face.

Sullivan must have come home and covered me with it. I'm not sure why. He could have just left me alone, but he made sure I was warm and comfortable.

He made sure I was okay.

A warm glow spreads over me. He cares about me. That's not in question. Why he does, I'm not sure. We hardly know each other.

Before I moved in last weekend, we hadn't spoken since college, and even then, we never interacted much. He was always around, courtesy of the small athletic department. We had a few classes together—I was a media design major, he minored in art. A lot of the core curriculum overlapped.

But we certainly were not *friends*.

I wasn't even friends with Josh back then. I knew him. He knew me. We didn't hang out. It wasn't until we reconnected at a New Year's Eve party that Sam threw that we even—

Sullivan was at that party.

twelve

. . .

Johanna: New Year's Eve

I DON'T KNOW what I'm doing here.

My neighbor invited me to her New Year's Eve party. I wouldn't have gone, but she's friends with an old teammate of mine, and I...

It's not like I had anything better to do on the last night of the year than curl up in the bubble bath with a bottle of orange soda and the newest Jenna McCall book.

Sam Burke has the misconception that we are friends. Maybe it's that we live in the same building in Everett. Or that her friend Diana was on the soccer team with me, and now that we have a truce, they've suddenly decided I'm fair game.

Either way, I find myself at this party, and I'm just... I'm not a loner, I've always had plenty of friends. It's just that since college ended and everyone went their separate ways, I've found it more and more difficult to keep in touch. Rachel and Rebekah are off in grad school, Robin moved to Nebraska for work, Rosie is back home in Texas, and I'm... here.

I didn't want to leave Boston. My parents are in Chicago— my dad teaches at Northwestern—but they didn't insist on me coming home, and frankly, I'm glad for that. I didn't want to go backwards.

I didn't want to stagnate, either, though.

Barrett Zhang comes over to my spot by the window, offering me a grin. "Hey, Jo," he says, nudging my arm. "How've you been?"

"Good. Great," I tell him with a bright smile.

Barrett snorts. "Yeah, tell me like it really is."

My fake smile falls. "I'm..." I sigh. "I don't know. You know?"

To my surprise, he nods. "Yeah, I do."

I had a crush on Barrett for ages. He's *Barrett Zhang*, star football player and the younger son of the wealthy Boston Zhang family. My parents would have been so proud if I'd been able to marry him.

But he's very plainly in love with Diana, my old frenemy and teammate, and after I pushed him into admitting his feelings for her, we've struck up a tentative friendship.

I don't know if I was ever actually interested in *him* or in what he represented. It's not something I like to think about. I was shallow, I was vain, and I treated him like an accessory rather than a person.

That's not the kind of person I want to be.

"How's the gig at Pluck?" he asks. His brother's business school friend runs the multi-media company, and my connection to the two of them helped me get the job as an entry-level graphic designer.

After the way I treated him—*especially* after the way I treated him—I owe a lot to Barrett Zhang.

The reminder of that makes me uncomfortable, so I shrug. "It's a job. It pays the bills."

Barrett smothers a snort. "Yeah, but it's a *job*. You get to do what you love."

He's stuck working at his family's forensic accounting firm, which he has made no secret about hating.

Luckily, I didn't have a family business to fall back on. My father is a philosophy professor and my mother is a mid-level executive for a major international grocery superstore. She has the social cachet to get me an entry-level job at her company—but I never wanted that.

So I stayed in Boston. I had the whole world open to me, but I didn't want to leave. I was comfortable here.

It helps that a few people I knew are in the same neighborhood. Sam and her old softball teammates live on the third floor, and they've mentioned some dude from the volleyball team is moving in two buildings down, and there are some former cheerleaders who are on the next street over.

I'm not alone here. In theory, at least. I'm not alone.

Barrett and I chat a bit, and then Diana comes over, and we force small talk for a little while. All it does is make me exceedingly aware of how uncomfortable I feel. My skin is itchy and my face is hot and I kind of want to crawl inside a hole and never come out.

It's not Diana's fault, though. It's just how I feel around most people. I never experienced it with Barrett, so I thought I must have feelings for him.

I need space. I need air. There are too many people in here, and I can't—

I just can't.

Winding my way through the party, I catch sight of Josh Sinclair, a giant from the volleyball team. He was on the student-athlete disciplinary committee along with me and Sam our senior year. We… aren't friends, exactly. But I could comfortably call him an acquaintance.

"Hey, Johanna," Josh says, giving me a nod. "Didn't think I'd see you here."

I roll my eyes. "Yeah, I'm full of surprises."

He doesn't give up, though. He follows me a few paces over to the drinks table, where I survey the options. Nothing looks good. It's not all alcohol, but none of the options are appetizing. In the end, I grab a bottle of water, and so does Josh.

"So..." He trails off.

"I'm not going to sleep with you," I tell him.

Josh chokes. "Excuse me?"

"That's why you're talking to me, right? It's an hour before midnight and you have to find someone to go home with for the night." I huff. "Well, it won't be me, so move along."

But Josh shakes his head and laughs. "I actually wanted to talk to you—just talk, no other intentions," he insists.

"Oh."

"I promise not all guys are dirtbags who only want to get into your pants." His eyes drift across the room to Sullivan, a football player who's wrapped up in an armchair with one of the sorority sisters. "Don't get me wrong, some people are. But I'm not that type."

After a while, I went up to the roof to get some air, and it seemed I wasn't the only one.

thirteen

. . .

Sullivan: New Year's Eve

I **CAME** to this party to get away from my life. It didn't work.

Escaping to the roof helped, though. The stark wind blows right through me, reminding me I'm alive. I have to remember that this discomfort is temporary. It'll fade. I'll be okay.

There's a fire pit with a circle of couches surrounding it. Why the hell did they crush fifty people into a tiny three-bedroom apartment when we could have partied up here?

A blast of wind rushes through me, and I realize why. It's fucking cold. It's the last day of the year, a few hours to midnight, and the temperature is hovering just above freezing.

Pulling my coat tighter around me, I lean against the handrail, looking down at the neighborhood below. The building is five stories, in a walkable neighborhood, and the kind of bougie hipster place Theo and I made fun of when we were kids.

But then—

Then Johanna steps out onto the roof, and I…

My brother always makes fun of me for my so-called

totally obvious crush on Johanna Chen, but—well, he's a dick, so I don't feel bad about punching him.

Sometimes.

But seeing her looking all chummy with volleyball douche Josh Sinclair made my blood boil. It doesn't matter that I was on the verge of hooking up with the hot blonde pre-med sorority sister. I just—I can't.

I've been in love with this girl for five years. Maybe it's crazy, because I hardly knew her back then, but it was instantaneous for me. Sure, it may have started out as lust. That was definitely why I asked her out at the freshman athletic department mixer our first weekend on campus.

"I'm not going to sleep with you," she'd said in that snide, sarcastic tone of hers, and I fell.

Head over heels.

I don't think she remembers that. I don't think she knows who I am, really. We've had some art classes together, but we've never talked. We run in different circles, even though we have friends in common.

She stops in her tracks at the sight of me. Her cheeks are flushed a violent red, a furrow between her brows.

"What are you doing here?" she snaps.

"Needed some air."

Her eyes narrow.

"I'm just hanging out," I add. "We can exist in the same space for a few minutes, right?"

"I can join you?" Her voice is snide, like she can't be bothered with my feelings on the matter, like she's going to do it anyway, regardless of what I think.

She's brazen, confident. Nothing fazes her. She's… steady.

"Of course." My voice cracks, and I cough to cover it. "How've you been?"

She narrows her eyes at me. "Since when?"

"Since graduation?"

That was the last time I saw her, at a frat party. Not that I'd graduated—I'm still on the five year plan, and I'm not complaining about that. A lot of my friends and teammates had moved on, so I went to say goodbye to them.

Johanna finished college in four years, balancing school and her commitments to the soccer team, serving as captain the last two seasons. It's admirable. I can barely manage to keep up with my schoolwork during football season.

Although...

Football is over now. At least for me. I've played my last season of eligibility. Now there's nothing to distract me from the vague emptiness of my life stretching before me.

What am I supposed to do now?

I can't keep pretending like hooking up with every woman who looks at me twice is fulfilling that itch inside of me. I want *her*. None of them compare, and I'm tired of lying to myself. Everyone wants a piece of the football player and the playboy, but nobody ever wants me for anything more than one night.

That usually suits me just fine, because all I ever want is one night. When Johanna realizes I'm right in front of her, everything might change... but she's made it clear she's not interested in me, so I'm not going to curl up in a ball and pine over a woman I can't have.

Even if I want her.

I told myself it was better to have someone than nobody at all. I thought I could distract myself from the pain of losing her, not that I ever had a chance with her in the first place.

And I'm not even close to being on her radar.

"I'm fine," Johanna says, lifting her chin.

"What are you up to?"

She glares at me.

"Job? You majored in art."

She scoffs, turning away.

"Hey, I'm genuinely asking." I reach for her elbow, then pull back. I can't keep chasing her.

"My major was Multimedia and Design," she says stiffly. "I'm working in graphic design."

My heart pounds. "That's awesome!"

She rolls her eyes at my genuine enthusiasm.

"That's really cool," I tell her sincerely. "I'm glad you found a job in your field. I'm hearing that's hard."

She shrugs. "A friend got me the job."

"Yeah, but you're *keeping* it. You're doing well enough that you can stay around." I shake my head, amazed. "That's the proof. Who cares how you got there? You're proving your worth now."

All of my friends were recruited into the athletic department. Newton *wanted* them. Somebody wanted them enough to take a chance on them.

I didn't get that. I was admitted to Newton because my mom works there, and I walked onto the football team. I was a three year starting player. Nobody does that these days. Most guys work out for a season, get zero minutes of playing time, and then quit the team.

I almost did. I almost gave up.

Even though I'm going through the pain now of losing the team, I wouldn't give up my four and a half seasons with the team for anything. If nothing else, it kept me in school. It kept me focused. Even though my season is done, I still have to keep my grades up if I want to stay in athletic department housing next semester. It helps motivate me.

Otherwise, I'd have to move home and live with my parents for my last semester of college. I can't imagine that being fun—for anyone involved. I don't think my brother would appreciate me asking to crash on his couch.

I thought I slept around a lot. I've got nothing on my brother. He has a new guy begging for his dick all the fucking time.

Shaking my head, I try to focus on the moment: the most

beautiful woman I've ever met, glaring at me in disgust like I'm scum on the bottom of her shoe.

"How's life on the other side?" I ask. "After being done with school?"

Johanna scoffs. "Why are you even talking to me?"

Fuck, that gets me hard. Every little scrap of attention she throws my way pulls me further into her web.

It started out as something physical. I was attracted to her from the moment I saw her across that party—long legs, muscular thighs, wide shoulders, and a fire in her eye that promised pain for anyone who crossed her.

Through the years, though, I've realized that's her mask. She's not comfortable being surrounded by people, so she pretends to be someone else.

I get that. Fuck, I've been doing that my whole life.

Fireworks crack in the distance. It's only nine o'clock. I don't begrudge their celebrating early. I'd join them if I could. I really don't want to go back down to the party, to the sorority sister I've been chatting up. It just seems so… pointless. Why should I brother pretending I want someone, when the one I want is up here with me?

There's a chance. It may be slimmer than a singular piece of paper, but there's still a chance. I can't give up yet.

Leaning down, I press a soft kiss to her cheek.

"Happy New Year, Johanna."

fourteen

. . .

Johanna

SULLIVAN KISSED ME. How could I have forgotten that?

Trudging out of my room, I make a quick stop in the bathroom, then head to the kitchen in search of coffee. Caffeine will make everything better.

I stop.

Sullivan is in the kitchen.

Shirtless.

Sullivan is in the kitchen, shirtless, cooking pancakes.

"Good morning," he says brightly, looking over at me. His eyes widen, no doubt taking in my terrible bedhead and mismatching pajamas. "Did you have a good sleep?"

My eyes narrow. What's he trying to pull?

"Or should I not talk to you before coffee?" He grins. "There's a fresh pot, and breakfast will be ready in a few minutes."

With a soft grunt, I pad through the small kitchen. My fuzzy sock-covered feet slip and slide on the vinyl flooring. Pulling down a mug from the cabinet, I fill it and sigh as the familiar scent washes over me.

Sullivan twists, opening the fridge and pulling out a bottle of peppermint mocha creamer. I could drink this shit year-round. In fact, I do.

But I ran out two days ago, and I haven't had a chance to run to the grocery store and pick up another bottle. In fact, I skipped my morning coffee entirely yesterday because I didn't have any creamer.

"Did you buy this?" I snap, peeling off the foil cap.

He nods, humming. "It's your favorite."

How does he know that?

"Should I have gotten a different flavor?" he asks. "French vanilla, or maybe salted caramel? That sounds good."

My brain is stuck on this. "You bought coffee creamer?"

Sullivan looks at me over his shoulder, confused. "Yes? It's a household necessity, isn't it?"

Pouring it into my mug, I inhale the scent and take a sip. "Yes. It is."

He grins at me.

Suddenly, I remember my manners. The bottle wasn't opened yet. That means he didn't get any.

"Do you want some? I can top up your cup."

"Oh. I'm good. I don't drink coffee," he says lightly.

He doesn't drink coffee? But every morning, there's a fresh pot made when I get up, waiting. It's not on a timer—my cheap machine isn't capable of that.

What the fuck?

He slides two pancakes onto a plate, then pours more batter onto the pan.

"You can get started, if you'd like." He pushes the plate in my direction. "Here, take this."

I glare at him. "Why are you being so nice to me?"

To my surprise, Sullivan laughs. "I'm not. This is, like, baseline courtesy."

"But..." I rub my forehead. "Last night... I just walked out."

"I shouldn't have pushed you." He flips a pancake,

focusing on the pan in front of him. "Have you ever heard of burnout?"

"What, like being stressed and overwhelmed?"

He nods. "Usually, there's a specific trigger. Something that causes it."

"I'm not stressed," I tell him, even though I know I am. Money is tight—I can *not* afford those books I bought last night—and I can barely breathe some days. Work is hard, and I don't have friends, and I just…

"Burnout can look and feel like different things," Sullivan says. "ASD burnout happens when you're struggling with the pressure of functioning in a neurotypical world, when life stress interferes with your coping strategies for social and sensory triggers."

"ASD?"

"Autism spectrum disorder."

My brain gets stuck on his word choice. "You have autism?"

He looks over his shoulder at me. "No. I don't."

"Then…"

Sullivan pulls the last two pancakes off the pan, then flips them onto a plate. He adds some scrambled eggs, then grabs a bottle of syrup and moves past me to the table.

I'm standing still, trying to process. I don't understand. What is he insinuating?

Looking over his shoulder, he catches sight of me, and with a smile, he comes back to me and takes my plate.

I start, pulling it back. His grip is forceful yet gentle as he removes it from my grasp, then puts it on the table beside his.

It's only then that I notice the table. There's a second plate with two sunny-side eggs—my favorite—with a bowl of cut fruit and a platter of turkey bacon.

"What is this?" I ask, as Charlotte jumps up onto her chair, and he puts a little scrambled egg and a small cat-sized pancake square on her placemat.

"We're having breakfast," Sullivan says, like it's obvious.

I rub at my forehead. "I'm confused."

"Food will help," he says firmly, kicking out the seat beside him.

"We're having breakfast," I repeat. He's watching me carefully, his expression guarded. "Thank you. You didn't have to cook for me."

"I wanted to." He spears a blueberry out of his bowl. "My mom is a psychologist," he says out of nowhere.

I blink. "Okay?"

"She earned her doctorate studying neurodiversity in people assigned female at birth," he continues.

"Isn't that women?"

Sullivan shakes his head. "Someone can be assigned female at birth and be a trans man or nonbinary. Her research now is on the queer experience in neurodivergence—anyways," he says, spearing another blueberry, "I'm familiar with neurodivergence in all its myriad representations and expressions, and it wouldn't surprise me if you were neurodivergent."

"Excuse me?"

"It's a broad term," he continues. "Neurodivergence includes things like ADHD and OCD and bipolar in addition to Autism Spectrum Disorder."

"So you think I'm on the spectrum?"

"Most autistics prefer to be called autistic since it's a defining quality of personality and existence." His eyes are guarded. "It wouldn't surprise me, though."

Squeezing my eyes shut, I try to make sense of all of this. "But wouldn't I know?"

He shrugs. "Sometimes. Maybe not. The definitions have changed over the years. And ASD in girls wasn't even thought to exist until recently. A lot of the traits are things that appear socially beneficial to young girls. There's more information now than there was before."

I stare at him. "So… what? What is the point of all of this?"

Sullivan tilts his head, looking at me. "Life is hard," he finally says. "But some people are playing the game of life on level four, and some are forced to play life on level forty-three. And that's hard. So, if you are, or even if you aren't… I think you deserve to at least look into the possibility. So you can get as much support as you possibly can."

"I don't have… that." I can't even say the words.

"Autism isn't contagious. There's a genetic component to it, sure," he says patiently. "It's not a disease. It's just… a fact of life. And more and more people are learning about it, which is a good thing. And if you're experiencing burnout, you're probably so overwhelmed by everyday life that the little things are pushing you over your limits, and if that's the case…" He sighs. "I just want you to have the support you need. Whether it's this or not, whether it's generic burnout or something more, we all deserve to receive support."

"I'm fine," I tell him.

He grins, shaking his head. "I didn't say you weren't." He looks at me seriously. "But there's so much more to life than being *fine*. That's what I want for you. I don't want you to be fine. I want you to be happy."

fifteen

. . .

Sullivan

SHE'S CONFUSED. Processing. I sit there patiently as she thinks. This is a lot, especially if the possibility has never crossed her mind.

"I'm happy," she says.

"Okay."

"I am," she insists. "I would know if I wasn't happy, wouldn't I?"

I shrug. "Sometimes. Or you might need somebody else to point it out. Usually I'm struggling internally for a while before anyone else is able to recognize it, but once they verbalize their concern, I am able to self-evaluate and put the pieces together."

She toys with her pancakes, chewing the inside of her cheek.

"It's okay to not be okay, and it's okay if you need help, too."

"You're struggling?" she whispers. She sounds lost.

"Not at the moment, though I did have a rough patch about six months ago," I tell her honestly. "I was unemployed for a good while after graduation and that really impacted me mentally. And then once I got my job, I had a long learning curve figuring everything out."

"It's just…" She sighs heavily. "It's hard."

Leaning across the table, I take her hand in mine, offering her strength any way I can.

"My job is—I mean, it's a job, I'm not supposed to like it," she starts, then sighs again. "But work sucks, and money is tight, and I have no life and no friends, and I just…"

"Okay, first of all, you have friends," I correct.

She scoffs.

"Diana?"

"She tolerates me," Johanna dismisses.

"Barrett cares about you."

She rolls her eyes.

"Josh asked you to stand up in the wedding," I continue. "And didn't Sam and Miles, too?"

She shrugs.

"And what about me? Aren't we friends?"

Johanna laughs outright. "You don't want to be friends with me."

"Don't I?" I squeeze her hand.

She's right, though. I don't want to be her *friend*. I want to be more. I want a life with her.

But if she's not ready for that, I'll take what I can get, and I'll enjoy every little scrap of attention and affection she's able to give me.

"There's that romance book club," I add. "Maybe you can find a rec soccer league, or a different sport, or a running club."

She scoffs again.

"I'm not trying to fix you. I'm trying to offer you solutions."

Johanna pins me with a flat stare. "Why?"

"Because I care about you," I say immediately.

"Why?" she asks again.

I squeeze her hand. "Why what?"

"Why do you care about me?" She rolls her eyes. "I'm just —I'm not worth it."

"That's where we'll have to agree to disagree," I return steadily.

She rolls her eyes, clearly disbelieving me.

My stomach sinks. There's no way she's ready for a romantic relationship, not if her self-image is this poor.

"I can't be the reason you change your life around," I tell her. "I don't want to 'fix' you. I want you to be happy, and I'll do everything in my power to make that happen. You can make friends with my friends, you can join me in my hobbies, but I think you need to find your own, too. You need to stand on your own two feet."

Johanna pulls her hand away from mine, crossing her arms over her chest. "I don't know how to do this."

"How did you and Josh become friends?" I've always wondered.

"We're not," she says immediately.

It's my turn to roll my eyes. "You're his best friend."

"I don't know why he thinks that, I barely know him."

"You guys get together at least three times a month for dinner and drinks," I remind her. "You've been friends as long as he's been with Theo."

She shrugs.

"He helped you move."

"Didn't you say that was basically a requirement for former athletes?" She narrows her eyes at me. "It's just— he's..." She runs a hand through her hair. "We served on the student-athlete disciplinary committee together. So I *knew* who he was. But I don't know him. We met at a party about a year after graduation."

"You asked him to help you rather than letting me do it," I point out.

"That's just because I know him slightly better than I know you, a virtual stranger," she says hotly.

My whole body feels like it's been zapped with a cattle prod, tearing a hole in the muscle that is my heart.

"We're not strangers," I say quietly.

Johanna scoffs. "Hey, guy I don't know who I'm living with now, can you please give me a towel because I'm naked in your apartment?" She rolls her eyes. "Yeah, that's a great impression on day number one."

"Okay, that was then. This is now."

"I don't know what you want me to say." She chews the inside of her cheek. "I don't…"

"You don't let anyone get close to you," I say quietly, holding her gaze. "You think you don't know people because you don't let them get to know *you*. You don't always know how to relate to people unless it's a competition, and then your focus is on being the best, so you don't have to make friends. But Johanna—it's okay to let your guard down. It's okay to let people in."

She looks away. "It's not that easy."

This time, I smile. "I didn't say it was easy. I said it was okay."

"Why do you care?" She glares at me. "Why does this matter?"

"Because I want you to be happy," I tell her again.

"Nobody is that selfless," she scoffs. "What are you getting out of this?"

"I can't want my friend to be happy?"

Johanna scowls.

She's not ready. It's clear she's not ready for what I want—what I *need* in a partner.

I want an equal. I don't want to be a caregiver. She needs to feel steady and sure in who she is and what she wants, and I don't want to shove her out of her comfort zone before she's ready.

But I also can't keep pretending.

"Look, I like you," I say lightly.

She squints at me. "What?"

"I'm not going to beat around the bush or act like I don't. I like you. But you aren't in a place where I would feel comfortable acting on that, so—for now—I just need you to accept that I want you to be happy, I want the best for you, even if that's not aligned with what I personally want for myself."

Johanna opens her mouth, then closes it. "I'm confused."

"Okay." I stack my dishes and silverware, then edge the empty plate away.

"You don't even know me," she says.

"I know enough."

"But—"

"We've known each other since we were eighteen. We met freshman year," I remind her. "We were part of the same athletic department for years. We have friends in common. We've gone to parties together."

She lifts her chin. "So?"

"So, I like you. I know you enough to like you as a person." I shrug. "I've been waiting long enough, and it's not going away. I'm not going to act on it; I don't want you to be uncomfortable living here, I just think you deserve to know. I'm not entirely altruistic."

"So what do you get out of this?" she demands.

"Well..." I sigh. "Hopefully, you get to a place where you would feel comfortable starting a relationship."

She laughs.

And then when she sees I don't join her, she stops.

"You're serious? You want a relationship?" She pauses. "With *me*?"

I nod.

"Why?"

"Because I think you're awesome, and I think we could

have something really great together," I say honestly. "What reason do I need?"

Johanna blows out a breath. "Look, if you're just trying to get laid—"

I cut her off. "If I wanted to get laid, I'd go to the bar or hit up an app and find someone for the night." My tone is blunt, and she winces, but she doesn't look away. "That's not what I want."

"You? Seriously?" She rolls her eyes. "You've never—"

"I've never dated anyone, because the one person I wanted to be with didn't have any interest in me," I say steadily. "At the freshman mixer, I asked you out. You turned me down. What, I'm supposed to harass you until you give in? That's not cool."

She stares at me. "The freshman mixer?"

"The first week on campus, freshman year. The athletic department threw a mixer in the ASC."

Guarded, she nods. "I remember."

"We were over by the snack table, and I asked you to dance, and you said off the bat you wouldn't sleep with me." I smile at the memory. That was it. That was the moment for me.

"I thought you were just hitting on me," she admits.

"I was."

She raises her eyebrows. "So..."

"So I was attracted to you immediately, and I wanted to get to know you. But you put up walls, and I wasn't about to tear you down for my own benefit."

Johanna scoffs. "And then you spent the next however many years screwing every girl who looked your way?"

"I wasn't going to obsess over you. I didn't think there was a chance, so I lived my life." I shrug. "I was single, I didn't date. I never led anyone on. There were always clear boundaries. What's wrong with meaningless sex with random people if the only person you're interested in won't give you the time of day?"

She opens her mouth, then closes it. "So what's changed?"

"Nothing's changed."

She frowns.

"You're still not in a place where we could start something meaningful, so no, nothing's changed," I repeat. "When you're ready, I'll be here."

Johanna swallows. "And if I'm never ready?"

I smile softly at her. "I'll still be here."

sixteen

. . .

Johanna

FOR THREE WEEKS, I go about my life.

Work.

Workout.

Read.

Sullivan changes his after-work schedule and we start doing our workouts in the basement gym at the same time. I do my best to keep my eyes on my own workout equipment… but I do add more squats into the rotation. Then we go upstairs, and some nights he cooks dinner, and some nights I do, and some nights we order in.

We sit on our separate couches, and I read while he sketches and watches sports on TV. I don't know what he's drawing, he never lets me see. He always asks what I'm reading, though.

It's… weird. I know that he likes me, but he's not *doing* anything about it. I guess I expected him to do something, to make the first move.

I haven't said the words out loud. I've searched online, sure. I've fallen down the hyperfixation rabbit hole of self-diagnosis and taken dozens of tests online, and they all return the same result:

There is a significant likelihood of autism spectrum disorder.

What I don't like is they won't definitively tell me YES or NO. It's always couched in scientific language. Probability. Possibility. Maybe.

YES. Or NO. Tell me one way or the other.

The other side of this… what do I do with these feelings Sullivan supposedly has? What, am I supposed to wait until I'm magically fixed and whole before—okay, first of all, autism is *not* a disease, and there's no cure.

I know he doesn't want me to change, per se. He just wants me to be in a healthy place. I'm not sure what that means, though. And I'm afraid to ask.

There's a crinkled piece of scratch paper on the fridge. He's taped it to the door because magnets won't stick to the surface.

The bookstore's romance book club meets tonight. This morning, he put two bottles of orange soda on the counter next to a six-pack of beer. BYOB was circled in black marker.

I know I should go. I know *he* wants me to go.

But I don't think I want to go.

I won't know anyone, and I'm always so awkward around new people, and they always think I'm a stone-hearted bitch, and then when they find out I like smut instead of *erudite literary fiction* they dismiss me, and—

At five forty-five, there's a knock on my bedroom door.

"Johanna," Sullivan says through the door. "Are you coming?"

Taking a deep breath, I fasten the last buckle on my boot and crack all of my knuckles.

"Come on," he adds. "It'll be fun."

I open the door and glare at him. "I don't think I like your idea of fun."

Sullivan grins at me, and my stomach flutters. "You're going to love it," he declares.

Grabbing my bag, which has my e-reader, two novels, and the bottles of orange soda, I pull on my favorite leather jacket.

He lets out a low whistle.

"What?"

He shakes his head.

I glare at him. "No, what is it?"

"Damn, girl," he says, his eyes roving over me in a caress more intimate than hands ever could be. "You're hot."

Rolling my eyes, I scoff. "Shut up."

I'm wearing normal clothes—jeans, a gauzy blouse I wore to work, and platform boots. My hair is in its regular ponytail, I didn't even freshen up my makeup. What is he seeing?

"Johanna."

Sullivan catches my arm as I try to move past. When he says my name with that hoarseness in his voice, I have to suppress a shiver.

"You look really great," he says, his eyes locked on mine.

I want to flirt with him, to test how serious he is. But that feels like crossing a line. I don't want to play with his emotions. He deserves better than that.

"Thank you," I finally say, and his grin lights up his face.

He squeezes my elbow. "Come on. If it's a bust, I'll take you out for ice cream."

I roll my eyes again. "What are we, ten years old?"

"Baby, we can get ice cream any time you want," he says.

A warm glow washes over me. He called me *baby*. Not in a mean, you're such a baby way, but in a protective, possessive, *you're mine-I'm his* kind of way.

I've never had that before. My previous relationships were always transactional and primarily physical.

I think I like it.

"I'll hold you to that," I manage, lifting my chin to hide how much I like this new side of him.

"You can hold me anytime," comes out of his mouth, and I blush, looking away.

Fuck. I don't think he was supposed to say that out loud.

Sullivan grins, and this time, I shiver all the way down to my toes.

There's a spark in his eye, and he leans forward. I almost think he's going to kiss me. The cedar of his cologne hits me, and I take a quick inhalation of that sharp, spicy scent that's come to haunt me every time I see the bottle on the bathroom counter.

I think I might want him to kiss me.

I open my mouth, tilting my chin up, trying to silently tell him it's okay if he does.

But he reaches past me and closes my bedroom door. The sharp snick of the doorjamb is like a shock to my system.

"Don't want Charlotte getting in there," he murmurs. He tucks a loose strand of hair behind my ear, then presses a lightning-quick kiss to my cheek.

Heat pinpricks at the point where his soft lips made contact with my skin. I want to—

Sullivan takes me by the hand, pulling me towards the door. "Come on. We're going to be late."

This is new. This version of him, forward, confident—this is not the way he's been with me for the last few weeks. It's like a switch has flipped inside of him, and he's all of a sudden decided to...

To what?

Flirt?

Pretend?

He releases my hand to lock the front door to the apartment, and I take the chance to hurry down the short flight of stairs before he can do it again.

I don't know what this is.

Does he think this is a date?

I swallow. Do I want him to think this is a date?

The walk to the bookstore takes about ten minutes. It's the longest ten minutes of my life.

Sullivan keeps pace with my quick strides, laughing under his breath when I tap my foot impatiently at the waiting crosswalk.

"It's going to be fine," he says.

"What is?"

Like it's not obvious why I'm freaked out.

He shakes his head. "You're going to meet people. You might even meet your new best friend. And if you don't—hey, no pressure. Tonight doesn't have to be the start of forever. Tonight can just be tonight."

I fall silent.

As we reach the bookstore, he opens the door for me, his hand on my lower back guiding me inside. I like this version of him. He's not just trying to get laid. He really cares about *me* as a person.

It's weird.

I'm not used to it.

But I think I like it.

I think I like it a lot.

There's a group of women seated in a circle at the back of the store. The cashier he was flirting with last time we were here is wearing her purple smock, chatting with a woman with dark, curly hair.

I can do this.

She catches sight of us and approaches. She's wearing a white sticker HELLO MY NAME IS name tag, which is good, because I've already forgotten hers.

"When I said it was BYOB, I meant beer, not boyfriend," Sadie says, glaring at Sullivan.

"He's not my boyfriend," I tell her quickly.

He laughs. "Thanks, Johanna."

Sadie smiles at me. "He just wants to be."

I choke. Sullivan's cheeks go pink, but he doesn't deny it.

"Do you want me to stay?" He asks quietly.

"I'm fine," I say automatically.

He laughs under his breath. "I know you're fine," he says. "Do you want me to stay?"

I *want* him to stay. I want him to be here.

But I don't *need* him here. I can do this on my own.

I shake my head, and he smiles at me, his hazel eyes warm and bright.

"Okay. Theo and I are grabbing dinner down the street. If you need anything, call me, okay?"

Biting my lip, I nod. It does make me feel more secure knowing he's nearby.

He leans forward and pecks me on the cheek. "You've got this," he whispers.

My face flames.

"Ooh, girl," Sadie says. She grabs my arm. "We'll take good care of her," she assures Sullivan, who winks at me. "Come on, I want to hear everything," she says to me, dragging me towards the circle.

"Everything? About what?" I ask.

"You've got a real life book boyfriend," one of the women in the circle says.

I open my mouth to object.

"Come on. Johanna, he said?" Sadie asks.

I nod.

She leads me over to a card table, where there's a pile of blank name tags and some baked goods nestled in among several bottles of alcohol. I slap my name on a sticker and put it on my chest.

"Let me introduce you to some people," Sadie says.

She seems to have made herself my new Sullivan—my new...

Hold up. Wait.

My new *Sullivan*?

She's just watching out for me. Making sure I'm okay.

The way he does, too.

My heart doesn't pound when she takes me by the elbow,

though, not the way it does when he's around. Her perfume is neutral, and it doesn't impact me like his soap in our shared shower does. I don't want to get closer to her, I'm fine in my personal space bubble, even though I like it the rare times he invades mine.

My stomach sinks like a stone.

This isn't good.

"Oh, fuck," I whisper.

"What is it?" asks one of the other women, sitting close enough to have heard me. Her name tag says Arielle, and she's holding a bottle of moscato.

I look over at her. "I think I like him."

"Isn't that a good thing?" she asks.

"I thought so," I tell her. "But now I'm really not sure."

Sadie snaps her fingers. "Do you drink? You need a drink."

I'm ushered into a chair beside Arielle, and she holds the bottle of wine out to me.

"What do you like?" she asks. "We've got, like, ten bottles of wine, beer, vodka…"

My mouth goes dry.

"Tequila," I murmur.

That'll fix it.

Sadie snaps again. "I like you."

seventeen

. . .

Johanna

BEFORE LONG, I have a red plastic cup of tequila in my hand.

"Sorry we don't have any good mixers," Sadie says.

"Don't need it," I murmur, taking a hefty swallow.

The burn hits me right where I need it to—in my cold, dead heart. I squeeze my eyes shut and try to focus.

Well, the good thing is, I'm so distracted by Sullivan's amorous intentions that I've forgotten to be nervous.

Fuck. Maybe that's why he did it. Maybe he wasn't serious about it. He just wanted to distract me.

I take another sip of tequila.

There are steps behind me, and two women approach, both holding a bottle of wine in each hand. A cheer goes up on the other side of the circle.

"Okay, now the party can start," cheers one of them.

My hackles rise. I don't know how to do this. I don't—

"What do you like to read?" Arielle asks me.

I chew the inside of my cheek. "Romance," I mutter.

She rolls her eyes with a smile. "Well, no shit, it's a romance book club."

On my other side, Sadie laughs. "Be nice. This is her first time."

"A virgin?" A perky blonde woman approaches. "Don't worry, we'll be gentle."

"Lots of lube," adds another woman with hot pink hair.

My face flames, and I lift my chin and narrow my eyes at her. "I'm not a virgin."

"But you're new to us. That makes you fun and exotic." Sadie winks at me. "Where are you from?"

I bristle. Is it because I'm visibly Asian? I don't want to be *exotic*. I want to be accepted for who I am, not what I look like.

"I've lived in the Boston area for seven years," I say coolly. "I grew up in Chicago."

"No way!" Arielle says. "Me, too!"

For a second, I don't know what to do.

"I'm from Highland Park," she adds.

"My dad teaches at Northwestern," I say. "My parents live just outside Evanston."

"That's super cool," Sadie says. "Maybe you've met in a different lifetime."

"I went to school in Connecticut," Arielle continues.

"We went to Michigan," the redhead in the corner chimes in. I squint at the sticker on her sweatshirt. Bex. "We were on the lacrosse team together."

She gestures to the woman beside her.

"Hail to the fucking victors," says the blonde with a wry grin. Vanessa, her name tag reads in flowing cursive letters.

She's pretty. Tall, too, with an athletic build. Her simple white t-shirt, jeans, and boots do little to hide the muscle tone in her arms and legs.

"I played soccer at Newton," I divulge.

Arielle groans. "No!"

Cautious, I look over at her. "Yes?"

She rolls her eyes. "Just when I thought I'd made a friend, I've lost you to the sportsball people."

I pause. "You want to be my friend?" I whisper.

She blinks. "Uh, yeah?" She sounds confused.

"Why?" I take a drink of my tequila. The burn warms me from the inside out.

"Because you're here," Arielle says. "We're friends now."

I narrow my eyes, trying to understand. I don't think it's the tequila making my head fuzzy.

"We like romance books," she says, gesturing to the room at large. "We're here to talk about books. You're here. That automatically means you're one of us."

I've never experienced this kind of unconditional acceptance before.

Even with all the soccer teams I've been on—and there were a *lot* of teams over the seventeen years I played—it was always a competition, jockeying for playing time, fighting for goals. There was a strict social hierarchy, and I was never on the top.

Except for when I was the captain at Newton. For a brief moment, I was at the top of the pyramid.

And then Diana came along and…

Well, whatever. She and I are okay now.

Sadie claps her hands, and the five side conversations stop.

"Let's go around the circle, introduce ourselves with our name, our current read, and our favorite trope." She grins. "I'm Sadie, I'm the manager of the bookstore, I'm currently reading Sybil Hedgewick's new alien book, and my favorite trope is enemies to lovers."

"I love Sybil Hedgewick," I blurt.

"She's so great," chimes Bex. She grins at me. "Hi, I'm Bex. I'm reading every book written by Ella Haines and Jenna McCall, and my favorite trope is only one bed."

The group goes around the circle. Vanessa likes sports

romance where he falls first. Kiley likes beauty and the geek. Elsy likes best friends to lovers. Ceci likes brother's best friend.

Arielle swallows beside me, and when it's her turn, she introduces herself with, "I like femdom," and then immediately hides her face.

"Yes, girl," Elsy chimes in, clapping.

"Get it, get it," Ceci adds.

"Oh, she does," Sadie says. "We're roommates. You should hear the stuff she gets up to with her boyfriend." She fans herself theatrically.

Arielle shrugs, her cheeks pink. "I like what I like…"

"And does he like it?" I ask, drawn in almost by accident.

She bites her lip, looking down. "He's certainly not complaining."

"Is that before or after the ball gag?" adds Kiley.

Arielle presses her lips together and looks away. "No comment."

The group erupts into good-natured cheer and laughter. I actually feel like I'm in on the joke, though. They're not making fun of her—they're happy for her, celebrating her good fortune.

I wonder what Sullivan would think of a ball gag…

Reaching for my cup, I gulp down the tequila. It burns as it goes down, and I start to imagine other things going down my throat…

A bolt of arousal strikes me dead between my legs, and I shift in my uncomfortable chair. That's new. That's different.

I've known that Sullivan likes me.

I've known that he's attractive.

But I haven't given thought to whether *I* like *him*.

I mean, as a friend, as a roommate, I like him. I get along with him. I might even go so far as to fuck him—because let's face it, he's gorgeous, and if his reputation is even halfway close to being true, he knows how to make a woman feel good.

But do I want the things he wants?

Sadie nudges me with her elbow. "Your turn," she whispers.

"I'm Johanna, and the new thing I'm into is books with neurodivergent representation," I finally say.

Arielle squeals. "Oh my goodness, there's definitely not enough! We'll have to compare TBR!"

"We have a whole table in the front," Sadie chimes in. "I'm trying to curate the selection."

I squint at her. I can't tell if she's being genuine or not. I don't really understand this dynamic. It doesn't make sense.

These people—some of them are former athletes, like me. Arielle is from my hometown. And Sadie…

I just don't know what to make of it.

Rather than most book clubs, where everyone all reads the same book and discusses it in depth, this seems to be a general free-for-all appreciation of romance novels. Not that I'm complaining. It's not what I expected, though.

There are about twenty women gathered tonight, mostly in their mid-twenties and thirties, with a few who are a bit older than that.

They all like romance novels. They come in all shapes and sizes, all sorts of hair colors, skin tones, and ethnic backgrounds, married and single, with families and child-free. There are two other Asian women, three other former college athletes, and at least one (Arielle) is from Chicago.

These are my people.

Privately, I make a note to research recreational soccer teams in the area. Sullivan mentioned it in passing, and I know Diana is part of a team. I don't necessarily want to join *her* team, though. I kind of want to have a fresh start on my own, unburdened by anyone's expectations of me.

I don't know what to think about him. He's… not what I

expected. When Josh suggested moving in with Theo's brother, I thought he would be more like Theo; loud, opinionated, outspoken, a little sexually aggressive, maybe kind of a slob.

But Sullivan is—

He's sweet. He cares. And I don't know how much is because of his so-called crush on me and how much is just who he is as a person, but I like it. I like that he cares.

He checks in on me. He makes sure I'm okay every step of the way, and he's there if I need him, but he also respects that I can and want to do things on my own.

Taking a sip of my tequila, I tilt my head, thinking of the things I'd like to do *with* him rather than on my own. My vibrator has been getting a workout lately. I could use some new batteries... unless he'd like to help me out.

Hm. Now that's an idea...

eighteen

. . .

Sullivan

"YOU'RE PATHETIC," my brother informs me, shooting me a dirty look.

"I know."

After checking my phone four times in five minutes, I've given up all pretenses.

"Johanna can take care of herself. She's not some shy, meek little—"

"I know she's not," I snap. "She's awkward and uncomfortable, so she's direct, but she's insecure about that, so she covers it up by being even more brusque, and that kick-starts her entire self-doubt cycle all over again."

Theo sips his drink. "Wow. You've really got a read on her."

I shrug. "I've been paying attention to her for years. Even when nobody else knew, I was keeping an eye on her. Now everyone just knows that."

"But you're not, like…" He makes a rude gesture with his hands.

"No. We're not sleeping together. I want more than that."

He sighs. "Oh, Billy."

"Don't call me Billy," I snap.

I hate that nickname. It doesn't bother me as much when my mother uses it. Coming from Theo, though, it feels like a taunt.

Then again, that's because it usually is. He knows how to get under my skin.

"When are you going to get off your fucking high horse," Theo snarks back.

I recoil. "The fuck did you just say?"

"You heard me," my brother snaps. "You told her you have feelings for her and you just—you don't pursue them?"

"It's a lot for her right now," I defend. "She's still coming to terms with the autistic burnout and the actual ASD itself."

Theo rolls his eyes. "I think that's just an excuse."

"Because I want her to be able to feel comfortable with who she is before we start a romantic relationship?"

"Self-actualization is a pipe dream," he says.

"But—"

"You can't put your entire life on hold waiting for her to magically pop up and say, 'Look, I'm functional, I'm good.'" Theo scoffs. "Jo's not like that."

"That's because she's masking."

"Exactly. And you're going to have to work *with* her to figure out who she is without the mask. She doesn't know yet. I don't think she's able to separate it."

"I just don't want her to be... dependent isn't the right word," I explain helplessly. "I don't want her to use me as a crutch. If something happens between us, and then it doesn't work out for whatever reason, I don't want her to be in a worse place than when we started."

"That's the risk of love," Theo shrugs. "As much as we try, we can't always leave the other person's heart intact."

"It's not about her heart. It's about her head."

"And maybe you two can grow together," he points out. "You don't have to grow like a vine by yourself. You can do it with the support of a partner, leaning on them, and then thriving in your own right."

I scrub a hand over my face. "What do you know?"

"I know that I'm in a happy, committed relationship. I'm getting married soon, and you haven't had a girlfriend since you were in high school," my brother snaps back. "You don't let anyone in, you keep them at arm's length—just like she does."

"I do?" That's news to me.

Theo laughs. "Yeah, Billy, you do. You're so wrapped up in this hero-worship fantasy that you forget you have your own life to live, too. Sure, you have friends, you go out and get laid, whatever, but you're just—you need to work on yourself, too. You can't just wait for her to work out her issues. You need to be doing it, too."

"What issues?"

"Well, for starters, figuring out why you've put yourself through several years of waiting."

"Because I love her."

It's as easy as that.

Theo squints at me. "Do you love her, or do you love the fantasy of her?"

"I'm in love with her."

"The woman you've been living with for the past month—you're sure you're in love with her? And not just the person you thought she was?"

"Being around her makes me happy. I feel like the best version of myself when she's around. She makes me *want* to be better. I'm attracted to her—I have been since the moment we met—but it goes beyond basic lust. It's more. She's…"

Theo waits.

"She's it. I just know it," I finally say. "I love the way she snipes and snarks at me, and I love the way she thinks she's tough and confident, but she's really the biggest softy, and she's…"

"You're in love with her mask," Theo tells me. "Not with her."

"Well, fuck." I sit with that realization.

Am I?

Do I even know her well enough to be in love with the true Johanna?

"Just go for it, dude," my brother encourages. "Try it out. See if it works. If it doesn't, well, at least you won't be in limbo forever. You'll know."

With a hum, I drain my beer.

I'm not sure I want to know.

Johanna has been this unavailable, unattainable jewel on the horizon for years, just out of reach. She's always been there. I've always known she's there and she has no interest in me. It's one of those constants, one of the truths I've memorized.

I don't know that I'm ready for that to change.

My brother walks me back to the bookstore, clapping me on the shoulder as we reach the double doors.

"It'll be okay, Billy," he tells me.

With a good-natured huff, I shove him away. "Yeah, yeah."

He stops. "Seriously," Theo says. "It will work out. It might suck for a bit, but it will work out."

"Thanks, jerkface," I tell him, punching his shoulder.

His laughter rings out behind me as I enter the bookstore.

The front of the store is quiet, only a few stragglers shopping. The party is in the back of the store, where about twenty women are gathered.

All of my attention narrows to the one woman I'm here for.

She looks happy. Her cheeks are pink, and she's smiling instead of grimacing, chatting with a brunette with curly hair. She sips from a red plastic cup, closing her eyes as she swallows. Her tongue comes out to lick a drop from the corner of her lips, and my insides go haywire.

Johanna smiles when she sees me, and my heart stops.

Do I love her, or do I love her mask?

Can the answer be both?

"Oh, look," calls a woman with hot pink hair. "It's your boo."

There's some good-natured laughter, but she doesn't seem put off. Johanna picks up her bag and approaches. Her movements are uncoordinated and unsteady.

Three feet away, she stumbles, and I rush to catch her.

"I'm drunk," she laughs, falling into me. Her arms wrap around my waist.

"You are." Holding her steady, I help her find her feet, and she leans on me, snuggling into my neck. "How was book club?"

I've never seen her this fluid, this carefree. Even when she's relaxing at home, she holds herself stiffly. Around Josh, she might shove him or nudge him, but she doesn't give him *hugs*.

I don't know what to make of this new development.

"It was fine," she says. She pushes her hair out of her eyes with uncoordinated movements. "Why won't you fuck me?"

Ohhhhh fuck.

"Yeah, dude," demands a redhead behind her. "Why won't you fuck her?"

I. Want. To. Die.

"Let's have this conversation at home," I tell Johanna, ignoring the other person.

Sadie meets my eyes. "You'll take care of her?"

With a nod, I hold my roommate closer. "Always."

One of the women in the background sighs, and another gulps down a nearly full glass of wine.

"I want that," a third one says, almost sadly.

I don't pretend to misunderstand what she means.

Because I want it, too.

With Johanna leaning on me, I help her walk the three and a half blocks to our apartment. She smells good, and I can't stop myself from holding her tight, because I know this is it— this is my chance.

If I don't do this, I never will.

If I don't try, I will kick myself for the rest of my life.

The chill in the air helps her regain some steadiness. She's able to walk up the stairs unassisted, and I stare at her ass like a lovestruck idiot.

With a shake of my head, I climb the stairs behind her, unlocking the door and ushering her inside.

She strips off her leather jacket and hangs it on the hook by the door, then unzips her killer boots. Without the help of the heels, she loses about three inches, putting the top of her head in line with my shoulders.

Johanna glares at me. "Did you have a good time?"

"Yeah. It was good to see Theo." I shrug off my coat, hanging it beside hers on the coat rack, and just the simple domesticity of it warms me through. "I'm happy he's happy, but I miss him sometimes."

She squints at me, trying to process this.

"I think you should fuck me," she announces.

I nearly jolt out of my skin. "What?"

Hands on her hips, she repeats: "I think you should fuck me."

"How much have you had to drink?"

"I know my limits. I'm consenting," she snaps.

"That's not what I'm asking." Pacing around the small living room, I try to work through everything from the evening. "Why do you want to sleep with me?"

"What kind of question is that? I want to sleep with you. Does it have to be more than that?"

My heart aches. She doesn't want me. She just wants a warm body.

I won't let her treat me the way I've treated all the other girls. They all knew they had no chance. I won't accept that; I'm going to prove her wrong.

"Johanna, I'm not going to fuck you," I tell her.

She recoils, hurt creasing her face.

"I want to be with you, I want to have something real with you. I want more than meaningless. I want every meaning there is."

Crossing her arms over her chest, she glares at me. "So then why the fuck haven't you done anything about it?"

It's my turn to flinch back.

"You say you have feelings, you say it's been years, but you've never tried to ask me out. What?" Her eyes are dark and hard. "You got rejected once freshman year and couldn't handle the idea of it happening again? Is that it?"

I shake my head. "No, because you're working things out. You're not ready for—"

Johanna sneers at me. "I think I know what I'm capable of."

Fuck.

Fuck this.

Fuck her.

Just… fuck everything.

"If you don't want to do this, fine," she snaps. "Just don't make up empty excuses. You had your shot. You wasted it."

Turning on her heel, she stalks off towards her room.

With a few quick paces, I meet her there. Her athletic body is pressed to mine, her curves as tantalizing up close as they were from across the room. Her mouth drops open, and she glares up at me, an angry set to her jaw.

Crowding her in, I push her back against the closed door. I cup her cheek with my hand and bring my lips to hers.

I kiss her.

I kiss her like it's the first time, the last time, the only time.

I kiss her breathless, stealing away those last few millimeters between us.

I kiss her like I have to leave tomorrow, like I don't know the next time I'll get to see her.

But mostly I kiss her like I've been wanting to since the day we met when we were eighteen and knew nothing. I still know nothing.

Well, I know one thing:

I'm every bit in love with her now as I was back then.

nineteen

. . .

Johanna

HOLY FUCK.

I can't breathe, can't think. Sullivan is kissing me, his lips soft and insistent against mine. I'm not usually a fan of kissing. It's too mechanical and I always overthink it and feel awkward.

If this is what it's supposed to be like... whew. I don't think I've ever been kissed properly.

It takes a second for my brain to reboot, and when it comes back online, I grab at his arms, pulling him even closer to me. His hard chest surrounds me, his spicy scent as comforting as ever. It sends a bolt of fire straight through me.

Sullivan pushes his thigh between my legs and I let out an embarrassing whimper as he rubs against my clit. His lips smile against mine, soothing away my mortification.

He likes this.

He likes me.

I don't know why, but he does.

He touches my face, my hips, my waist, and I remember that I'm supposed to be an active participant in this, too. My hands move to his hair, sinking into the blond-brown waves.

Sullivan groans deep in his throat. He hitches my leg up

around his waist, his hand coming up to cup my ass as he thrusts against me. I can feel him hard at my core, and my eyes roll back in my head as he grinds into me right where I need it most.

His body is firm against mine, solid, his presence enveloping me. I've forgotten why I was upset, forgiven him for making me goad him into action.

I could do this forever. I never want to let him go.

But all too soon, he's pulling away, leaving me breathless, my mouth open and lips swollen.

"Good night," he whispers, giving me one last, soft peck. I moan, trying to pull him back, but he stays out of reach.

I watch as he walks backwards towards his room, like he can't bring himself to look away. He lingers in the doorway.

There's a scratch behind him, and we both look down to see Charlotte's paw beneath the door, trying to claw her way out of his room.

The moment shatters.

"Good night," he says again, opening his door and closing it behind him.

What the hell was that?

It takes me a moment to kick my brain into gear. As I run through my nightly routine, taking off my makeup, brushing and tying up my hair, my skincare routine, I think about how silly this all is. Am I supposed to pretend I'm not thinking of him? He's *right there*. Our bedrooms share a wall.

As I brush my teeth in our shared bathroom, his bedroom door stays closed, and it's only once I'm back in my room that I hear him open it and take his turn in the bathroom.

I put on my sexy-time playlist and pull out a book and my favorite toy. The buzz of the tequila has burned off, leaving me buzzing with a different kind of stimulation. And I don't think he's willing to help me out tonight.

He doesn't want to fuck me? Fine. Then he can listen as I get myself off.

Most nights, I try to be discreet. I'm not trying to hide, I'm not ashamed of taking care of my own needs, but I'm not making a big show of it, either.

Tonight? I don't care what he thinks.

But even with the help of my favorite book and my favorite toy, I can't reach satisfaction. The orgasm leaves me empty, unfulfilled. I want more. I *need* more.

It takes longer to get there the second time. I'm not trying to make a big deal of it, but I just need to get *off*. And I don't care that it's a toy and not him—I just need *relief*.

But even a second orgasm doesn't help.

With a groan, I roll over in my bed, rubbing my face. There's an itch beneath my skin, a restlessness in my blood that I can't tamp down.

Sighing, I pull out the big kahuna, a different toy that usually gets the job done in two minutes or less. Just the sound of the motor makes the slickness between my legs start up again.

The door to my room bangs open, and my heart jumps.

"What the fuck," Sullivan demands. He's standing in the doorway, shrouded by the light of the hall.

He stops, his mouth agape.

I'm laying naked in my bed, the blankets kicked to the foot of the mattress, a giant black dildo half inserted inside me. The buzz of the vibrator is loud in the quiet stillness of the room, and as the vibration hits a crescendo, I can't help but squeeze my eyes shut and whimper. It's too much, it's almost painful, but I can't get *there*.

Sullivan stares.

I'm naked in the most pure sense of the word, but his eyes strip me bare even without fabric in the way. He sees me, sees *inside* of me, in a way I've never experienced before. His eyes pin me to the spot, my shoulders glued to the mattress as my hips ride the toy.

"Fuck," he whispers, scraping a hand over his cheek, before he strides forward.

Before I know what's happening, he's crawling onto my bed, approaching me like a panther in the night.

Capturing my cheek in his hand, he kisses me roughly, his tongue thrusting between my lips. I open immediately, yielding to him in every respect. His groan reverberates through me, the sound eclipsed only by the buzzing of the toy between my legs.

"You okay, baby?" he murmurs.

I shake my head. "I can't—"

"Can't what, Johanna?"

My name sounds like sex in his lust-hoarse voice, dripping from his tongue like honey.

Grabbing for his shoulders, I try to pull him down on top of me. But he holds himself up, not letting me maneuver him. The only clothes he's wearing are a pair of loose shorts which do little to disguise his hard, thick cock.

"What do you need?" His thumb strokes my cheek tenderly.

"I need you."

Sullivan lets out a shaky exhale.

"I need you," I repeat, my voice more steady. "I can't get— *unh*—I can't get there."

"Baby, I heard you come. I heard you call out." His thumb traces my lips, and I draw him into my mouth, sucking around the digit. "You've got to stop torturing me this way."

"Torture you?" I laugh around a moan. "I can't fucking get off, and you think I'm torturing—*ahh!*"

His hand snakes down my body, touching me between my legs. He grasps the handle of the toy and pushes it deeper inside my body. The vibrations intensify, winding me up and coiling me even tighter.

"Please," I beg, reaching for him again.

This time, Sullivan yields for me, letting me pull him half

on top of me. His hard body feels delicious on top of mine. He slides his other arm beneath me, wrapping me up in his embrace as his hand moves the toy inside of me.

I grab his wrist, and he stills.

Tightening my grip, I cling to him as my hips move, and he resumes his ministrations. He kisses me, his mouth sweet and promising dirty things to come.

I hope they're to come.

I hope I get to come.

The sensations of his knuckles maneuvering the toy against my thighs drives my senses haywire. I don't know how I've lived my entire life and not experienced this before. I don't know how I'm supposed to live the entire rest of my life and never experience this again.

With a sad whirr, the vibrator slows. I almost think he's doing it intentionally, but in that hard to reach part of my brain, I remember it was almost out of battery. I save it for emergencies because it takes so damn long to charge.

When the vibrations stop completely, Sullivan moves the dildo a few times in and out of me before I grunt and move his hand away.

"Not working?" he murmurs, tracing the toy along the seam of my legs, before sinking it back inside of me.

I groan in frustration. Tears prick at my eyes. I just *need*, damn it.

Scrambling for him, I pull his body on top of mine, trying to recreate some sort of the physical connection that I need right now.

"Johanna—"

His voice is hard.

I stop, releasing him.

Sullivan peers down at me. The streetlamp across the way illuminates the contours of his face, the hollows beneath his cheekbones and the faint scar bisecting his lip.

He's beautiful.

Not physically—I mean, yes, with his features, he's gorgeous, but he knows that.

Inside, in his soul—his heart is beautiful.

"I need *you*."

The words fall from my lips before I can stop them. I'm so tightly wound, I don't know that I'll ever be able to get relief again. He's the cure, the only one that can fix it.

Not a toy.

Not anyone else.

I need *him*.

Sullivan groans. He touches his lips to mine in the faintest whisper of a kiss before he pulls away.

"Ride my cock," he says, rolling to his back. "Use me, take what you need. I'm yours."

Scrambling up, I straddle him, and at the first contact of his fabric-covered dick against my sensitive skin, I let out a rattly moan. His hands fall to my hips, tightening almost painfully, his fingers digging into the top of my ass.

His eyes are wide as he drinks me in. The moonlight casts its silvery light across the bed, illuminating his pale skin, his tattoos dark against the lighter flesh of his broad chest.

He's hard and thick beneath my core. My hands fall to his pecs, squeezing the firm mounds of muscle for balance as I start to ride him, dragging my soaking wet cunt along the line of him.

Sullivan is breathing hard, his eyes locked on mine as he thrusts up against me, as if he's trying to bury himself inside of me even with the fabric of his shorts in the way.

"You feel..." Inhaling sharply, I twist my hips, trying to find the perfect amount of friction and the exact right angle to bring the most critical amount of pleasure.

"You like this?"

His voice is rough, gravely, and the rumbly sound sends goosebumps along my skin. My nipples bead into tight buds, and with a groan, he moves a hand to my breast, cupping me there. His thumb rubs over the pebbled point and I let out a whimper.

With a grin, he tugs gently, and I nearly lose my balance. He releases my breast immediately, his hand returning to my hips as he holds me steady.

"Use me," he whispers. "I'm here for you."

I let out a breathy grunt as I swivel my hips, rubbing my aching clit along his length. I wish there were no clothes separating us. I wish there was nothing between us.

But if he wouldn't fuck me an hour ago, I don't think he will now. He might let me *use* him, but he's not *mine* to keep.

And I want to keep him.

The thought hits me suddenly, and I lose my grip on his chest. He slides his hand up my back, urging me down, and as I lower my chest to his, my tummy against his softer belly, I think that this is almost like being in his arms again.

He's holding me.

It's almost like a hug.

Which is—I almost have to laugh, because I would never have thought that I'd be the type of person to prefer a hug to a quick and dirty fuck. It's the kind of intimacy I've never allowed myself to indulge in. It hasn't been offered with much frequency before. Hardly ever.

My hand cups Sullivan's cheek, and he gazes up at me, adoration in his eyes. This is real for him. Whatever he feels, no matter my doubts of its veracity, he's sure.

I can't just *use him* and discard him. This means too much to him.

Slowly, gently, I bring my lips to his, and he opens for me immediately, his tongue coming to meet mine.

The first touch sends lighting bolts through me, and as his hands tighten on my hips and his hips snap up into mine, I fall.

I fall, and I didn't realize I'd been that high up, because I'm tumbling down and there's no end in sight.

But then he tightens his arms around me, grounding me. He's caught me.

No matter where I am, no matter how far I fall, he'll catch me. I know that for certain.

He kisses me softly as I come down from my high, his hips grinding into mine with less pressure now. One of his hands roves up and down my back, smoothing comfort into my sweat-slick skin.

"How're you feeling, baby?" he murmurs, his eyes hazy and half-closed.

"Mm." I let out a happy sigh and collapse against his chest, my head nuzzling automatically into his neck.

I'm not much of a cuddler—I've been told on several occasions that I'm as prickly as a porcupine after sex—but right now I want to be *inside* him, inside his skin, inside this moment. I never want it to end.

"Was it good for you?" His palm cups the back of my head, holding me close.

I nod against his neck. My lips ghost over his pulse point and I press a kiss there, and when he takes a sharp intake of breath, I suck gently.

"Are you feeling better?"

"So much." I feel drunk again—this time no tequila needed. I'm buzzed off the feeling of his sweaty skin pressed to mine, his fuzzy chest hair scratchy against the sensitive skin of my breasts.

There's a wet spot beneath me, and I think maybe I should be embarrassed about that, but I can't find it in me to be embarrassed about my body's natural reaction to him.

"That was so good," he murmurs, his voice hoarse. "I love what you do to me."

"Was it good for you? I just… I used you."

Sullivan huffs out a laugh. "Baby, you can use me anytime."

The wet spot is moving, and it's warm, and—*oh.*

He came.

In his shorts.

He came from me riding him.

With a yawn, I tighten my arms around him. "Mmkay."

His hand smooths over my back, his palm warm and heavy like a weighted blanket. I fall asleep still straddling him, wrapped around him like a koala.

But when I wake up, I'm alone.

twenty

. . .

Sullivan

I'M IN HELL.

Johanna is naked on top of me, fast asleep, and I'm in hell.

I never want this to end.

After that kiss… fuck. I waited for her to be in bed before I got into mine and rubbed one out.

And then I heard her vibrator start up.

And then I heard her moans.

And then I…

Well, I waited. I listened.

I can hear the vibrations most nights, likely when she thinks I'm asleep. She always turns on music to cover the noise, but it's a specific playlist she uses that isn't her bedtime playlist, so I always know when it's about to happen. Fuck, I've woken up out of a dead sleep before at the sound of it.

But tonight… she came twice. I heard her call out, I heard her moans, I heard her cries, and I wanted to be there. I wanted to be the one forcing those sounds from her.

Instead, I laid in my bed like a coward with my hand on my dick, touching myself as my roommate got herself off.

It didn't stop.

She didn't stop.

And then... well, I had to stop her. I had to barge in there before the sound of her vibrator stealing her pleasure was lost forever.

But that was then, and now she's asleep, and I'm beneath her, my shorts filled with my quickly drying cum. *Urgh.* The pleasure has already faded, leaving me feeling gross and slimy.

I took advantage of her. She used me, but I took advantage of her. She rode my dick until she got what she wanted, but I used her body, her voice for my own selfish pleasure.

I don't know how I'm supposed to look at myself in the mirror after this.

Gently, I roll her over onto her side, and she shifts in her sleep into a more comfortable position than with her legs wrapped around me.

Her soft breath against my neck is stimulating me in all the wrong kinds of ways. My heart races. What the hell did I get myself into? My breathing comes quicker now, and my hands start to shake.

I don't know if I can do this.

My world is crashing down around me, and I—

I wasn't prepared for this.

When I told her about my feelings, I used it as an excuse not to pursue her. I gave myself a reason not to act on it. She had enough going on.

I never let myself consider a reality in which she returned my feelings.

I never let myself consider a reality in which she didn't return my feelings.

Her own feelings just... didn't exist. Because they weren't *hers.* She didn't know about mine, so she couldn't have her own.

But tonight...

With a sigh, I pull myself from her bed, then pull the covers over her nude body. She looks so peaceful, so happy.

Before I can regret it, I press a kiss to her forehead.

And then I walk away.

Closing the door behind me, I head straight for the shower and climb in without waiting for the water to warm up. The cold might help me figure out *what the fuck did I just do?*

The shower doesn't bring me any clarity, though.

As I climb back into my bed, Charlotte curls up beside me, the robotic motor of her purr at a different pitch than the motor Johanna was previously using.

Fumbling for my phone beneath my pillow, I unplug it from the charger and unlock the screen, dialing the number one person in my favorites.

The line rings twice before a gruff, "What do you want, asshole?" sounds in my ear.

"I fucked up," I whisper.

Theo sighs. "It's two o'clock in the fucking morning. What did you do?"

"I kissed her." Squeezing my eyes shut as if that will help hide me from his scorn, I exhale slowly. "I did so much more than that. We..."

"Did you fuck her?" he demands.

There's a questioning noise on the other end of the line, and I know it's Josh.

"We..." I swallow thickly. "Okay, I was wearing shorts, but she wasn't, and she..."

"Billy," my brother says sharply.

"I just—I couldn't stop myself. I heard her and she..."

"Heard her?" Josh's voice is hoarse.

"Yeah. We got home and we were—she was drunk, and she was taunting me, and the next thing I knew I was kissing her, but when I realized what was happening, I walked away. And then she... I *heard* her."

Josh gulps. "Shit."

"Is that a bad thing?" Theo asks.

"It's not ideal," he answers. "The last actual boyfriend she had was junior year, and that didn't last long. She's dated a bit. It never lasts very long."

"I don't think I could handle it if we started and it didn't last," I admit.

"So we'll have to make sure it lasts," my brother says.

"How?"

Theo yawns. "I don't know, fuckhead. We'll figure it out later."

———

Morning comes several hours before I'm ready for it. At six, my alarm blares, and I stumble through my morning routine before grabbing the suitcase in the corner of my room.

It's a quick hour and a half flight to Baltimore that takes nearly half the day between travel time to Boston Logan, getting through security, waiting for the flight to board, then touching down in Maryland and making my way to the conference hotel.

I'm a coward.

I didn't even tell her I was leaving.

Granted, I found out yesterday at the end of the workday, and I was so focused on making sure she went to book club that I... conveniently didn't tell her.

It's only for two nights.

She'll be fine for two nights.

Right?

She's an adult. She's perfectly capable. Hell, she lived on her own for two and a half years. She'll be fine.

My chest pangs at the thought of her, and I glance down at my phone again.

She hasn't messaged.

Then again, neither have I. I don't know what to say.

Hi, I love you, but I don't know if I'm in love with you or the imaginary mask you use to hold the entire world at arm's length. Will you please have my babies?

Maybe it's a good thing I have this conference this weekend. I'll be able to get some space, recalibrate. I'll be able to process.

The Indie Writer's Association is one of the biggest organizations for independent authors to meet and greet. Unofficially, I'm there to get my publisher's name out there. I'm not an agent or an editor, but if I want to make my way up the ranks, I have to start familiarizing myself with both the writers and the competing houses.

Outside of the Big 5 New York houses are a dozen or so mid-market presses, and then there are plenty of independently owned publishing companies like mine. I'm fairly set on staying in Boston long-term, I have no interest in moving to New York, and it's too competitive up there for me to survive working remotely. It's all about who you know.

And I know my family is in Boston, so that's where I want to stay.

My parents are there, my brother is there, my friends are there... it's where I grew up, it's where I want to grow old. I just have to figure out what else my future will hold.

Checking into the conference, I wheel my suitcase to the elevator bay. I reach for the button at the same time as another hand does, and our fingers connect.

With a jolt, I flinch back, and a low, husky laugh greets my ears.

"Didn't think you were that much of a wuss," a woman taunts.

Turning, I see none other than Sadie, the bookseller from last night.

I frown. "What are you doing here?"

She raises her eyebrows. "Going to a conference. You?"

"Same." I glance at her name badge. *Sylvie Hirsch* is written on the tag. "Writer?"

She nods. "You?"

"I work for Cole and Pittman, I'm an analyst."

"Nice."

The elevator dings and she steps onto it, then looks back at me challengingly. Gamely, I join her, pressing the button for my floor.

"So the girlfriend…"

I sigh. "Johanna's not my girlfriend."

"But you want her to be?" she asks.

"Yeah."

Sadie laughs. "Because you have a little…" She gestures to the collar of her shirt.

"What?"

"You've got a love bite, dude. Might want to cover that up before you go home to the Missus."

Rolling my eyes, I shake my head. "Yeah, except she gave it to me."

She grins. "Nice!"

I shrug. "It should be, except she's there and I'm here and it's… hard."

"It's hard," she echoes. "Been there, done that, got the scars to show for it. It doesn't get easier."

"Nope."

On the echoes of my sigh, the elevator doors part.

"See you around," I tell her, lifting my hand goodbye.

"Let's get a drink later," she suggests.

I frown.

"I'll give you the scoop on book club last night. I'll help you woo her." She grins, and I have to laugh.

"Sure. Sounds nice."

As I trudge down the hallway to my room, there's a pep in my step that wasn't there before.

Asking my gay brother and his equally gay fiancé for relationship advice at two o'clock in the morning probably wasn't my best idea…

But getting a drink with my roommate's new friend and book club buddy? Yeah, that might work a bit better…

twenty-one

. . .

Johanna

I'M CONFUSED.

I've been confused all day.

Sullivan doesn't message me all day, and I'm certainly not about to be the one to break this stalemate and text him first.

Sorry for climbing on your cock and making you come in your pants?

Hard pass. Besides, I'm not sorry.

What's a girl to do but eat greasy food and drink cheap liquor?

I show up at the lobby of Josh and Theo's building with takeaway noodles, orange chicken, and broccoli beef. Even though my family grew up preparing authentic Chinese dishes all the time, I have a not-so-secret love for the giant Panda chain with restaurants in strip malls and college dining halls. It doesn't taste anything like the Chinese food I'm familiar with, but it's comforting all the same.

The doorman scans my ID and I take the elevator up to the eleventh floor. The door to their apartment is unlocked as usual, so I let myself in.

And immediately, I wish I hadn't.

Josh is naked.

He's on his knees.

His arms are tied behind his back with a pair of fuzzy handcuffs.

And he's…

He's getting his face fucked. That's the only way to describe it.

My face warms, and I can't—stop—staring.

Theo grunts, lifts his hand from Josh's hair, and waves at me. He's naked, his other hand fisted in Josh's hair as he uses the bigger man's face to get himself off.

"Didn't expect you," he pants, and Josh gives a little gurgle.

"I'm going to—I'm gonna go."

Turning around, I exit the apartment, making sure to close the door firmly behind me, and scurry back to the elevator. The doorman gives me a funny look when I rush out so soon.

Yeah… I'm going to need more than orange soda to scrub that from my brain.

There's a bar across the street. With a sigh, I head there. Usually I prefer to drink in the company of other people I know rather than strangers. I don't trust myself when I drink.

Case in point: last night.

Blowing out a breath, I open the door to the sports bar, and I'm greeted by a wave of stale body odor so strong the stench nearly bowls me over. *Urgh.*

No.

I can't do this.

Turning tail, I move to the café next door instead. It's a quaint little bakery with a picture of a cupcake on the door. It should be safe.

Right?

Ordering a cookies and cream cupcake, I set my rapidly cooling Chinese food on the table across from me. I can eat dessert first.

My phone vibrates with a text, and my heart jumps. Maybe it's Sullivan. Maybe he's—

It's not Sullivan.

But my heart jumps for another reason.

It's Arielle.

Before I left last night, she made everyone put their numbers into my phone, and I've never been more glad until this moment.

Hey, this is going to sound totally crazy and I promise I'm not a stalker but I'm at a bar in Fenway-Kenmore and could have sworn I just saw you. Are you around?

I look down at my cupcake, then pensively at the wall separating the bakery from the sports bar.

I'm next door, I type back.

Hold please, she types immediately.

I blink.

Hold what?

Returning to my dessert, I go back to digging the base out of the cupcake and leaving the puddle of frosting to eat last. Less than three minutes later, the door bursts open and Arielle comes through, her wild curls frizzy from the humidity.

She catches sight of me and beams.

"Hey, stranger!"

I manage a smile back. It feels more like a grimace, but I swear I intend for it to be a smile.

"What are you doing in this part of town?" Arielle tilts her head, studying me.

"My friend lives across the street." That's the best way to say it.

"Oh. So where's your friend?"

With a sigh, I dig into the cake of the cupcake. "Getting fucked."

She laughs. "Yeah, that tends to happen."

I shake my head. "Usually I don't have to see it, though. I

could have lived my entire life without knowing what his pale, hairy ass looks like."

Arielle grimaces, dropping into the seat across from me. "So you mean, like…"

"Literally. Getting fucked." I shudder. "He and his fiancé apparently don't lock their front door, even when they get busy."

"So you're here."

"I tried going next door, but the smell…"

"Yeah, it's a lot if you're not used to it," she agrees. "I'm glad I found you, though!"

"You are?" Why don't I believe that?

"Yeah. I had fun last night. Hope you did, too."

Arielle gives a small smile. Her eyes dart around the bakery and she's practically vibrating.

"I did," I admit quietly, inclining my head. "I'm glad I went."

"We'll see you next month?" she presses.

I nod. "That's the plan."

She beams at me. "I have to tell Sadie. She'll be so glad I didn't run you off."

"Why would you run me off?"

Arielle shrugs. "I can be intense. It's a lot if you're not prepared for it. But when I saw you, I just knew."

"Knew?"

"That you're neurodivergent," she says flatly.

I flinch.

Her mouth drops open. "Shit. Did I read that wrong?"

A part of me is aching for someone to talk to about this. How did she know? Is it obvious? Or is it something that only people in the cool kids' club can tell?

I can't answer her.

"Okay, well, I'm going back next door. The hockey game starts soon, and—"

Somehow, what comes out of my mouth is: "You're watching a hockey game?"

Hesitant, she nods.

"But you called it sportsball last night."

Arielle laughs. "That was for comedic effect."

I stare at her.

"You... don't do that?"

"No, I do," I admit. "I just didn't think other people did, too."

"Well, for me, it's because I'm awkward and on the spectrum and it's my way of trying to relate to the person I'm speaking with."

I feel like I've just been slapped across the face with a fish.

"You're on the spectrum?"

Arielle nods, like she can't believe I didn't know. "I like to call it neurospicy. Just a little hint of spice in an otherwise bland world," she grins.

"I was told... Someone said I might be, too. And I don't know what to do."

She takes a deep breath. "Okay. Well, first of all—it doesn't have to define you or mean anything if you don't want it to."

Picking at the peeled wrapper from my cupcake, I nod.

"For me... I was diagnosed because my social milestones weren't being met. I was verbal really young, and I was reading when I was four, but preschool and then kindergarten were rough. It was really hard for me. I think I was six or seven."

I blink. I didn't even know it could be identified that young.

"What did they do? To diagnose?"

She shrugs. "I met with a child psych for a while and they observed me, did a thorough questionnaire with my parents and my teachers. I couldn't verbalize a lot of my issues yet. I have a sensory processing disorder and was having meltdowns, and they thought I was just being difficult. It wasn't until the psychologist explained that I was getting so overwhelmed by the tags in the back of my shirt and the fabric of my sweaters and the ridge of my socks on my toes that I wasn't able to focus or comprehend anything outside of that. For me, it's usually a physical sense, and fabrics are a big trigger. For other people, it can be noise or smell or taste or all of them combined."

"And what, you just… take meds?"

Arielle shakes her head. "There's no meds because there's no cure. Nothing is *wrong* with me. I just don't process things the same way other people do, I need certain accommodations like taking the tag out of my shirt and wearing certain brands of clothes. Different isn't wrong. For so long, there's been a very strict definition of what's normal and acceptable. We're just starting to learn about other ways of thinking, of processing, of different needs. A hundred years ago, people like us were thought to be dumb if they were nonverbal. Or changelings as milestones weren't met. Or geniuses and savants. But they made exceptions for people in their families, 'oh, it's just how they are, and it was fine.'"

"And now?" I'm at the edge of my seat, hanging onto every word.

"Well, we're so digitally connected. We can't hide. And we know more. Different doesn't mean bad. It's just… not what they're used to."

"I didn't understand it," I admit. "I still don't know that I do."

She shrugs. "I've had almost twenty years of knowledge, and it still surprises me. Like, I forget that some things aren't a universal experience. But I also hang out in a lot of spectrum-focused spaces online, so I'm able to connect with people like me even if they don't live near me."

My eyes are wide. "There are—"

"Girl, you have no idea." Arielle grins. "Okay, let me get a cupcake, and then we'll go into the details. You're about to get dumped into one of my current hyper-fixations. It's great."

Forcing a laugh, I watch as she goes to the counter and orders a cupcake for herself and a coffee.

"My parents took me to a child psych when I was a kid," I tell her.

She blinks.

"I don't really know why, and they never talked about it. Do you—do you think they knew?"

She tilts her head, thinking. "Well, there are many reasons you could see a psychologist. It could be behavioral or academic or anything else. In the 80's, autism was thought to be really rare, and in the 90's, it was increasingly recognized, but even twenty years ago, boys were still five times as likely to be diagnosed as girls."

"What? Why?"

"Well, girls are socialized to withdraw, which is thought to be a good thing, whereas boys are given the freedom to have meltdowns and draw attention. They have the same hyperfixations and repetitive and restrictive behaviors, they're just viewed as socially acceptable. It's a whole thing."

"You know a lot about this. I'm sorry to be asking you so much. I just..."

"Don't worry about it. It's one of my hyperfixations," Arielle waves it away.

"My... friend."

"The one getting fucked?" she says slyly.

"No. Well—okay, one of them," I amend, "Theo was the one doing... Anyways, my friend from last night."

Arielle's eyes brighten. "The cute book boyfriend. Yes. I remember."

"His mom is a psychologist." I try to recall exactly what Dr. Sullivan-Caldwell studies. "Something to do with neurodivergence in female something or other."

She nods. "That sounds fascinating. I'd love to pick her brain."

"Do you think… is that something I can do?"

"Well…" She bites her lip. "What's the situation with the guy?"

I glance at my phone. Still no messages from Sullivan.

"I don't even know half the time."

"Oooh, girl." Arielle digs into her cupcake. "Tell me everything."

And before I realize it, I do. It comes pouring out of me—why I moved in with Sullivan in the first place, the awkwardness between us, my meltdown over brunch and then the trip to the bookstore, that stilted dinner, the breakfast, the silence for three weeks…

And then the kiss.

My face heats at the memory of his kiss, the way his body felt against mine, how nice it felt to be in his arms. And then when he came into my room… I bite my lip, my body reacting immediately at the memory, and my core clenches around emptiness.

Fuck. I don't want to have another night like last night, unable to find the relief I so desperately needed.

The tinkle of the bell above the door to the bakery chimes, and I look up to see Josh in the doorway.

"Can we talk?" he asks, his face red. There's fresh beard burn on his neck and his mouth is swollen. I cringe as I realize exactly why I know his lips are swollen.

"Ooh, is this—?" Arielle studies him. "He's cute."

"*He's* also in a relationship," Josh says stiffly. "Jo, please."

"You really need to lock your front door," I tell him, shaking my head.

He rolls his eyes. "Or you can just knock before you come in."

Arielle snorts. "Okay, I'm going to leave you two to your lovers' spat. Have fun. And seriously, call me. We'll grab coffee or something next week. Maybe brunch with Sadie when she gets back in town."

"Sounds good," I say with a smile that actually feels genuine.

She waves at Josh as she leaves, and he slides into her seat.

"Do you want to talk about it?" he asks.

"I'd rather forget about it and pretend it never happened."

He cringes. "You're not, like…"

I shudder. "I don't want to see *anyone* naked or having sex. It has nothing to do with you or with Theo, your proclivities, or anything about that. I barely like looking at myself naked. There's a reason I can only have sex with the lights off."

He blinks. "Okay, yeah, not where I thought you were going with that, but we should probably unpack this."

Waving his concern away, I stand up to throw away my cupcake wrapper. "Let's go for a walk."

Exiting the bakery, we each zip up our coats as we're hit with a brisk wind.

"Why'd you come over? Not that I didn't want you to," he adds quickly. "I just wasn't expecting you. Normally, I'm the one reaching out to you."

"Sullivan and I fooled around last night."

Josh stops in his tracks. "What?"

"He kissed me," I add. "I mean, I goaded him into it, but he kissed me. And then later… there was…"

"I know what there was," he says quickly. "I don't need to know more."

It's my turn to stop. "Wait, how do you know? Did he tell you?"

My friend hunches his shoulders, like that will make the six-foot-seven giant seem smaller and less punchable. "He talked to Theo, and I overheard."

I rub at my eyes. "Wow. Okay."

"How is this different than you telling that woman, or you telling me now?"

"Arielle is—she's my friend," I say, and I'm surprised when I find the sentiment doesn't freak me out like it normally would. "You're my friend, too. Isn't that what friends are supposed to talk about?"

"Theo is his brother," he reminds me.

"So?"

"So they talk."

"And what did he say?"

Josh rolls his eyes. "Oh, no. We're not playing a game of he-said-she-said. You want to know, you pick up the damn phone and call him yourself."

twenty-two

. . .

Sullivan

THE CONFERENCE IS—WELL, it's work. It's networking. But it's surprisingly fun. After not expecting to be able to attend, I'm finding myself glad that Steve got the stomach flu. Usually, a junior analyst would never be invited to one of these things. The company had paid for the ticket and paid for the room, though, so it was easy for them to swap me in.

And I'm not going to waste a second of it.

There's a panel in the afternoon to kick off the conference, then a meet and greet with industry people in the hotel restaurant. I don't have any friends here, I've never been to one of these events before, and the only person I know—Sadie—has her own agenda for being here.

So, I get a drink—tonic water and lime, because I don't need to be drunk, I just need to look like I fit in—and then I start to mingle. As a natural extrovert, talking to people isn't hard. It is a little different when I'm trying to get their attention on my own merit, though, and they're not adoring the college football player who won the game.

I don't know how to balance this.

Small talk is one thing. Trying not to mention my

employer and subtly see if people are interested in contracting with us? Entirely different.

At dinner, I'm seated with reps from publishers. They're about a rank or two above me, not quite so green, and it's clear they've met before. As I sip my drink, I realize this could be me: next time, this *will* be me. I have to show them my best face, get them to realize I'm one of them, a peer. The group is evenly split between men and women, around my age in their mid-20's, though some are on the other side of thirty. They're just… normal people, who do the same types of things I do.

After that, it's a little easier to relax.

Sadie approaches after dessert is served. "C'mon, dude," she announces. "We're drinking."

I laugh, and one of the guys across the table looks over in interest.

There's no denying it, Sadie is hot. She's short and curvy with dark eyes and olive skin, a killer smile, and a rack the old me would have died for.

But she doesn't compare to Johanna—not in the slightest.

I was serious when I told her that I was just biding my time, waiting for her to be ready. Fuck, a week before she moved in, I was still hooking up with random women. The second there was a chance she would be back in my life? Yeah, I stopped all of that.

When I couldn't have her in my life, I needed the distraction. There was no hope of anything happening when she didn't know I existed.

Now that she's in my life… I don't even want to *think* about anyone else.

Settled in the hotel bar, I get a glass of water and Sadie orders a beer and nachos.

"Was that the most disgusting dinner you've ever had?" she says as she dips a cheese-covered chip into guacamole.

I shrug. "I've had worse." Helping myself to her nachos, I lean back in my seat and pull at my tie. "Had to go to a bunch of formal dinners in college. It was always rubber chicken and green beans. I *hate* green beans."

She laughs. "Bad dining hall food?"

"Nah, our dining hall was good. They spoiled us. It was the main university catering staff." I shudder, remembering the food poisoning everyone got after the end-of-year banquet my junior year. "They took care of the athletes pretty well."

Sadie looks me over in interest. "You were an athlete?"

"Played football."

"Huh."

I roll my eyes. "What?"

"You don't seem like the type."

"What does that mean?"

"You're not a loud-mouthed alpha asshole with an ego the size of Rhode Island."

I crack up. "Clearly you don't know me."

"The guy I saw last night at the bookstore? The guy who asked me about book club? You care about her."

"Not mutually exclusive. I can be a dick and still think with it." Catching the bartender's attention, I point at Sadie's half-drunk beer, ordering one for myself.

"So what's the deal there?"

"I like her, she knows, and I can't do anything about it until she figures out her shit." There. Succinct.

"What kind of shit?"

"The personal kind of shit that I won't be discussing," I tell her flatly.

Sadie raises her hands innocently. "Just trying to help."

"Yeah, well..." My beer arrives, and I nod at the bartender, taking a slow sip. "The question isn't if I like her, or even if she likes me. The question is if she's in a healthy enough headspace to start a relationship. I don't want to casually date. I want to *be with* her."

"Last night..." She points at my neck.

I run my fingers over the bruise I've memorized. "Last night was last night, and now I'm…"

"Do you regret it?" she asks bluntly.

I pause.

"Shit, dude. If that was a mistake—"

"Being with her was *not* a mistake," I say hotly. "The problem is…" I sigh. "The problem is, it wasn't this big, romantic gesture, I kissed her because I was pissed. How's that for you? I was annoyed and she was taunting me and I kissed her to make her shut up."

Sadie rolls her eyes. "Yeah, but you *wanted* to kiss her."

"I've wanted to be with her since we met when we were eighteen," I correct.

She blinks.

With a sigh, I lean back in my side of the booth. "I had all these ideas of how our first kiss would go, you know? There were all these expectations."

"Was it a bad kiss?"

I glare at her.

"What, sometimes it can be a dud. Doesn't mean there's no chemistry. It just needs kindling." She smirks. "Do you need pointers?"

"It was a fucking awesome kiss," I snap. "The problem isn't the kiss. The problem is what happened after, and then…" I rub at my eye. "I want to love her, not use her. And all she did was use me."

"Well, fuck." Sadie sips her beer. "I don't know if I have any suggestions, dude."

With a snort, I roll my eyes. "You don't say."

"May I offer you a piece of advice?"

"Might as well." It's my turn to smirk at her. "You probably can't make the situation worse."

"You might be waiting for her to figure her shit out, but you need to get yours figured out, too," Sadie says.

"What do you mean?"

"You didn't take advantage of her. She was throwing herself at you when you came to pick her up."

"Because she was drunk."

She rolls her eyes. "We watered down her tequila, it wasn't that strong. It was clear she had eyes for you—and only you."

"That doesn't mean—"

"She's not your manic pixie dream girl," she snaps.

I blink.

"She doesn't exist to make your life better or complete. She's not a side character in your story: she's the main character."

"I know that," I tell her quietly. "She's everything."

"But are you ready to be everything to her?" She pins me with her stare. "Or are you indulging in the fantasy of what you wanted for so long without having to face the fact that what you wanted was an idealized version of a real person with real thoughts and feelings?"

Picking up my beer, I drain half the glass.

"I don't think I like you," I say, copying Johanna, and Sadie grins.

"You're going to love me," she teases, and my heart stops and my face goes slack.

"This isn't—I'm not flirting with you. I'm serious about her."

She rolls her eyes. "Dude. Get real. I'm not hitting on you, just like you weren't hitting on me at the bookstore." She sits back in her side of the booth. "Do you ever meet someone and think—I need to have you in my life?"

"No?"

"I think you and I need to be in each other's lives," she says slowly. "We're… well, we're not the same, but we fit together. Platonic soulmates or whatever."

"Look, dude, I'm not…"

She rolls her eyes. "Obviously, that's pushing it. I'm not

saying it's love at first sight or anything, not like it obviously is with her. Men and women can be friends. I'm not attracted to you—seriously, man, you're not my type, and even if you were, I don't go after guys in relationships."

With a sigh, I rub my face, declining to point out that *technically* I'm not in a relationship—because I want to be, and I'm purposefully living my life in such a way that would be conducive to me and Johanna finally, *finally* getting together.

Sadie sits quietly. "I need a friend. And frankly, I think you do, too."

twenty-three

. . .

Sullivan

SADIE and I are three drinks in when my phone buzzes with a call. I check the display, and almost drop my phone into my beer when I see the name on the front.

Johanna.

Scrambling for the phone, I answer it immediately.

"Hey."

"Hi. Where are you?" Her voice is quiet, only a hint of insecurity in her tone.

"Listen," I start. "I should have told you."

"Told me what?"

"I'm—"

"Hey, dude," Sadie calls out from three tables away, where she's mingling with another group of conference attendees. "I need another drink. You good?"

"You're busy," Johanna says, that snide tone creeping into her voice. "I should go."

"No, wait—"

The line goes dead.

Shit.

Shit, shit, shit.

"I gotta go," I call back, scrambling for my wallet. Dropping some cash on the counter, I exit the bar and jog to the elevator. My bladder protests the quickness of my pace, the doors miraculously slide open, and I jab at the button for my floor several times like that will make the metal cage move faster.

I click on Johanna's name on my phone screen, but there's no connection in this metal cage.

As soon as the door springs open, I hit her contact again. The line rings once before it disconnects.

Fuck.

Letting myself into my room, I immediately take a leak, wash my hands, and splash some cold water on my face.

Okay.

I can do this.

We can do this.

We can make this work.

I call Johanna a third time, and now, the line rings and rings. I almost think she's going to let me roll to voicemail when the line connects.

"What do you want?" she snaps.

She's masking, hiding her insecurity behind a layer of bravado so thick, I don't think she can see through it.

"I want to talk to you." I keep my voice light and even. "I'm at a conference, and I should have mentioned it, but—"

"You're out with a woman," she snaps, her tone snide and sharp.

I blow out a breath. *That* is the part that bothers her?

"I'm at a work conference, and I was in the hotel bar with a—"

"I don't want to hear it."

"A *friend*," I yell.

Her sharp intake of breath hits me like a slap across the face.

"She's a friend, and she's trying to help," I say more calmly. "Your friend—Sadie, from the bookstore?"

"She's not my friend," Johanna says automatically.

"Yeah. Well, she's at the conference, and she's trying to help me fix things with you."

Assuming there's enough there to fix.

"Why didn't you tell me you were leaving?" Her voice is small. "I woke up and you were just… gone."

Scrubbing my hand over my face, I admit: "I thought if I told you I was leaving, you'd find an excuse not to go to book club last night. And I wanted you to enjoy yourself there."

"I wouldn't have…" She trails off. "Okay, so maybe I *might* have convinced myself not to go."

Swallowing nervously. "And then this morning…"

The line disconnects.

I stare at my phone. What the hell just happened?

Did she hang up on me?

My phone starts vibrating with a video call. My heart rate normalizes at her picture on the display.

"You hung up on me," I accuse as the call connects.

Johanna is sitting on my leather couch, Charlotte perched on the back of the sofa, with my green blanket wrapped around her. She looks—

Her eyes are tired, and there's bags under her eyes, but there's a smile on her face like the weight's been lifted off her shoulders.

"I needed to see you," she says quietly.

"You could have told me," I chide gently.

She tilts her head. "Really?"

"Yes. Babe, next time, don't just hang up, tell me you're—"

She squints at me. "There's going to be a next time?"

"I hope so," I tell her honestly. "I'd like there to be a lot more times."

Her face falls. "Because you'll be gone."

"I'll be back on Sunday. This trip is a blip. It's work."

She chews the inside of her cheek.

"I want *more* with you. I want all of it." There's no hesitation on my part.

"I want to meet your mom," she blurts.

My face goes slack. "Uh, what?"

She shakes her head. "No. I don't want to meet *your* mom. I mean, I do. I want to meet her. But you said she—I want to know what she's researching. I want to talk to her."

My heart rate slows ever so slightly. "Okay. I can arrange that."

"But I also want to meet her," she adds. "Because she's your mom."

"Johanna…"

"I made a friend. My new friend Arielle and I ate cupcakes today," she says.

I blink. *Is that a euphemism?* Hey, if she wants to explore a burgeoning desire for bisexuality, I'm all for it.

Running my tongue over my teeth, I ask, "How was it? Did it taste good?"

"It was fine. Sweet."

I press my lips together to hide my smile. "Where'd you go?"

"This little bakery in Fenway-Kenmore after—well, I was there, and she found me."

"Oh, you mean *cupcakes*," I realize. Like, the dessert.

Johanna blinks. "Yes?"

"What did you and Arielle talk about?"

She takes a deep breath. "She told me about her experiences growing up on the spectrum."

My heart hammers wildly in my chest cavity. "Yeah?"

"Yeah. Did you know boys are five times more likely to be diagnosed than girls?"

"I did know that, yes." I keep my voice even.

Johanna pauses, then exhales. "I didn't know. I knew I was different, but I didn't *know*. And she told me about all these groups and forums, and there are support services, and I—*I didn't know.*" Her voice hitches.

"I know, baby," I murmur. "You know now."

"It's like…" She pulls her hair out of her ponytail, the shiny strands sticking up from static. "I'm a zebra, but I've always been around thoroughbred horses, champion racehorses who won every race and competed at the highest levels. And I didn't know there were other zebras like me. I didn't know there was a community for zebras because I didn't know anyone else was like *this*. I just knew I wasn't a horse."

"You're not a horse," I confirm, my heart pounding. "You're exactly who you're meant to be."

"Right. And I—" She stops. "Thank you for telling me."

"Johanna…"

Distressed, she shakes her head. "I wouldn't have known. It might have taken me forever to put the pieces together, but now that they have, the puzzle is taking shape, and it makes *sense* in a way that it never has before. I can see the pieces the picture makes instead of all the little squiggly bits."

"I happen to like the squiggly bits."

She cracks a smile, and a lightness in my core makes me feel warm and fuzzy inside.

"I like *you*," she says.

My heart stops beating.

"I don't know what that means," she continues immediately. "I don't know what that means for us or what we do next, I just know that I like kissing you and I want to do it a whole lot."

In my dress slacks, my cock jerks, and I curse the four hundred miles separating us.

"I could get on the next flight. I could be home in a few hours," I offer.

Johanna laughs and shakes her head. "No. You're at the conference. You need to work." She pauses. "But next time, don't leave me naked and alone in bed without saying goodbye."

My heart leaps. "You want there to be a next time?"

Slowly, she nods. "I don't know how we do this," she admits.

"Do what?"

"This." She gestures between us. "You're... I don't date much."

"I don't date at all," I tell her honestly.

She squints at me.

"I took women home for a good time, but it never went beyond that. I never let myself catch feelings," I say with no hesitation or remorse. "I knew I wanted you, but I never thought it would happen, so..."

"I just want to make it good for you," she blurts.

"Baby, it's already good for me."

Johanna frowns.

"I get to see you every day. That's enough for right now."

"But the rest—I mean, we *live* together." She pulls at her hair.

"We do. And that means we'll have to have some conversations and figure out what that means for us going forward," I agree. "But that doesn't make me want to do this any less."

"I don't..." She takes a deep breath. "I don't know how to do this."

"Well, first things first," I say, toeing off my shoes and relaxing further on the bed. "How was your day?"

She blinks. "My day?"

"Yeah. You went to work and then met up with your friend?"

Johanna relaxes. "Yeah. I finished up a few projects today, so tomorrow should be a light day at the office. I went to—" Her face turns red, and she looks away.

"What?"

"I went to see Josh," she blurts.

My eyebrows rise. "Oh?"

"He was… busy," she says.

"Tied up?" I ask mildly.

She chokes, her face nearly purple.

"I know what Theo's into." I shrug. "He and Josh are certainly… compatible."

My brother is a power top who looks like a twink, and as Josh once described it, he's a greedy bottom who happens to be a physical giant. People usually assume the opposite to look at them, but as long as it's safe, sane, and consensual, it's nobody's business what they do behind closed doors.

The only problem is that they both have an exhibitionism streak. It's been a standing rule in the apartment that everyone has to wear pants in the common areas.

"Anyways," Johanna continues loudly. "I went to the bakery across from their apartment and ran into Arielle from book club, and we chatted for a bit, and then Josh came to find me and we went for a walk."

"How was it?"

She pauses, and my stomach leaps.

"Babe, you can talk to me," I tell her quietly.

Her jaw ticks. "Like you talked to your brother?"

Oh.

Oh, shit.

"Does that bother you?" I hold my breath.

She grinds her teeth. "I didn't like finding out that you told all your friends we hooked up."

"Okay, let's back up," I tell her, sitting up straight. "First of all, I didn't tell *all my friends*," I assure her quickly. "I went to my brother for help, because I was convinced I had ruined everything."

Johanna blinks. "Ruined it? How?"

"Because you were…"

"If anything, I'm the one who took advantage of you," she says blandly.

My cock jerks in my pants, and I adjust myself as I shift on the bed.

"Is that what you think happened?"

"Uh, yeah, I remember exactly what happened," she says with a flat monotone.

"So you remember me barging into your room and basically—" I shiver at the memory, my cock reacting automatically to the view of her wet cunt with a thick black dildo half-inserted.

"I couldn't come," she says, a hint of pink on her cheeks. "I mean, I made myself orgasm. But I couldn't *come*."

"You couldn't find relief." That puts a whole new spin on the interaction, and my brain spins as it tries to think this through. "But when we…"

"When I climbed on top of your dick and basically rode you like—"

I clear my throat, my balls heavy and aching. "Yeah. That."

She stops. "Do you not want me to talk about it?"

"I never want you to stop talking about it," I admit. "I just…"

"What?"

I groan. "I'm here, and you're there, and I can't *touch* you, and…"

"You're right," she says quietly. "You can't touch me, and I can't touch you."

Leaning back on the pillows, I wince.

"But I can touch myself."

twenty-four

. . .

Johanna

MY HEART HAMMERS wildly in my chest. Is this real? Am I really suggesting…

Sullivan's pained groan echoes in his empty room.

"Are you okay?" I ask immediately, all dirty thoughts forgotten.

"Johanna. Baby." He sounds like he's in pain.

"What?"

"Please tell me you're not suggesting what I think you're suggesting." His eyes are bright, his face flushed, a bead of sweat at his hairline.

He's not interested. He doesn't like this.

I didn't take him for a vanilla missionary-only with the lights off type of guy.

"Never mind, I can—"

"You want to touch yourself and I get to *watch*?" His voice cracks.

"Is that… something you'd like?"

His eager nod is answer enough, and his words punctuate it. "Yes. Absolutely. Yes. Please. Yes."

I look around the living room. I'm on his couch with his

blanket wrapped around me, but Charlotte the cat is right next to me, purring away.

I can't do this here.

"Hold on a second." I get up and waddle to my room as best I can wrapped up in his blanket burrito, closing the door and then locking it for good measure. Even though he's so far away and I'm home alone with the door locked, I don't want to chance anyone walking in on me, feline or otherwise.

Setting the phone down on my nightstand, I angle the camera towards my side of the bed.

"I think we need a new house rule," Sullivan says. "No more pants mandate. You can't wear pants in the common areas. No pants. Never pants."

Snorting out a laugh, I whip off my top.

He swallows, his Adam's apple bobbing in his thick throat. "Fuck," he whispers.

"Too much?" I'm wearing a camisole and a bra beneath my comfy house sweatshirt, so I'm still covered.

"Baby…" His slow exhale makes it seem like he's enjoying this. "Not too much. Never too much."

I bite my lip, considering the box of his photo on my phone screen. He's still dressed, his tie hanging loosely around his neck.

"Take off your shirt," I demand.

"You're bossy," he teases with a smile.

My stomach sinks. *I'm too much.* I'm going to scare him away.

Swallowing, I square my shoulders. This is me. If he doesn't like me as the way I am, I'm not going to pretend to be someone else for him. I'm not going to *mask* as he called it.

"I like it," he continues, pulling his tie from his neck. "You can boss me around any time you'd like."

A flash of lust strikes through me. "You'd like that?"

Sullivan nods readily. "Yes. Absolutely."

"Okay. Then take off your shirt *and* your pants."

With considerably more finesse than I did, he captures my gaze through the phone screen as he slowly slips the first button free, then the second, his fingertips grazing the column of his sternum.

I want to be there, touching his chest, memorizing the taste of his skin, the slight tickle of his chest hair against my breasts. My nipples tighten within my bra, and I drive my hand into my camisole top, pinching and tugging at the beaded buds.

He groans, his eyes locked on mine. "Take off your shirt," he counters, his voice hoarse.

Before I can move, he shifts on the bed. Stripping off the starched dress shirt, without further ado, he whips his plain white t-shirt over his head, leaving him bare from the waist up.

Dark hair covers his strong, broad chest, contrasting with his pale skin and tapering down into a thin line on his soft belly. He has a small tattoo over his heart, and I know from sitting across the table from him at breakfast a few weeks ago that it's a small football and an anatomically correct heart.

Ink covers his strong arms, a full sleeve on the right arm and a partial sleeve on his left. It reminds me of my own tattoos, of the stark lines of the flowers covering my shoulders and biceps.

I don't like the look of my body. It has nothing to do with being fat or skinny or muscular or petite. My strong muscles and thick thighs don't bother me. It's not vanity. I just don't like looking at myself naked. I never have. Bare, naked skin kind of freaks me out.

The lines of ink etched into my skin help with that itchy, uncomfortable feeling. It makes me feel grounded. The only reason I don't have a full body tattoo is money. I've been working on my shoulders and upper arms for the last few years as I've had the expendable income, which hasn't been often.

"Baby?" Sullivan is watching me, his head cocked. "You okay?"

Shaking my head, I force myself into the moment. "I'm good. I'm fine."

"I know you're fine," he says steadily. "But are you okay?"

"Yeah, I was… thinking. Thoughts. My brain was busy," I answer, gesturing to my head.

He's moving now, setting the phone down. There's a clink of jangling metal as he unbuckles his belt, unbuckling a pair of dress slacks that cling to his strong thighs.

Biting my lip, I watch with bated breath as he unzips his pants and kicks the fabric away. Beneath, he's wearing a pair of boring blue plaid boxer shorts, which are doing a poor job at disguising his interest.

"What do you want, Johanna?" His voice is like butter, and my mouth goes dry. His eyes are locked on mine as he runs his fingers over his soft belly.

"I want to taste you." The words come automatically. I want to know him, the texture and salt of his skin. I want him *here*, with me, right now.

Sullivan groans, squeezing his fist around himself. I can see the shiny head of his cock pressing up against the waistband of his boxers, and I want to wrap my lips around him and *suck*.

But I can't. Because he's not here. He's there.

Backing up a few paces, I kneel on the bed, then pull my camisole over my head. My plain, boring beige bra is—

Well, he's looking at me like he's just seen a miracle.

"What do I do now?" I ask. I'm still wearing my leggings, but I don't know that I'm brave enough to take them off on camera.

"Whatever you want to do," he says. He pushes his hand

beneath the waistband of his boxers and tugs them down, showing me his cock.

It's a pretty cock. If dicks are pretty, this one certainly is. I know his hands are giant, and from the way his hard, leaking cock fills his palm, it's proportionate to the rest of him. He's thick, too, with a swollen head that I want to suck on.

As I watch, he trails his fingers over the ridge of veins on the side of his dick. He gathers some of the wetness at the tip and uses it to coat his length.

Heat rolls through me, and I pinch my nipple through the bra. He groans.

"What do you like most?" His gaze is heated. "Do you like fingers, or do you prefer a mouth on your pussy?"

I swallow. "Um…"

"I want—I *need* to know how to get you off," Sullivan continues. "It's very important to me that you understand this. Your pleasure is my highest priority. If you're not satisfied, I'm not doing my job right."

Biting my lip, I whisper, "Fingers are okay. Mouth is better."

"I can't wait to taste you, to bury my face between your thighs and have you ride my face like you rode my cock last night."

A fresh burst of slick wetness at my core makes me shift and squeeze my thighs together.

"Fuck," I whisper.

"Yeah. That. I'm going to fuck your gorgeous cunt with my tongue until you come on my face," he says.

Heat ricochets through me, and frantically I push my leggings off my hips, so eager to get them off that I accidentally give him an up close and personal view of my tits. Before I can overthink it, I pull off my cotton panties, too, the gusset soaked through.

"Johanna. Fuck."

"Hold on."

"Oh, I'm holding on," he mutters, and I grin as I rummage through my nightstand. I had my collection of toys charging all day, so now they're ready to go. No more battery mishaps like last time. "What do you like most? What gets you in the mood?"

"I, um, I like toys. They help me get there." That and a very intense collection of one-handed reads on my kindle.

"I know," he says with a smirk.

I freeze. "You know?"

His smile is bright. "I can hear you."

"No, you can't," I tell him automatically.

"You have a special playlist that you use, and, well—your toys aren't always quiet. And neither are you."

My face flames, and I look away.

"I'm not complaining," Sullivan assures me. "Fuck, the number of nights I've laid there wishing I could join you…"

"You could have." I meet his gaze. "You should have."

"Next time, I will," he promises.

Finding the toy I'm looking for, a thick vibrator with a butterfly attachment, I add some lube and press the toy between my legs.

He blows out a heavy breath, squeezing his hand around his dick.

"Turn it on," he whispers, his eyes dark.

Clicking the button, I allow it to warm up, the vibrations slowly rolling through me. After a moment, I press it inside of me, canting my hips up. Letting out an embarrassing whimper, my eyes are locked on the image of his thick cock in his thick hand, every pass of his fingers over the shaft making me wish they were pushing inside of me.

Once the toy is seated between my legs, the silicone attachment pressed to my clit, I turn the vibrations up a level.

My moan is soft and breathy, and I see his cock dribble a fresh burst of pre-cum at the noise. His hand moves slowly over his length, smearing the wetness along the shaft as he reaches a hand between his legs to cup his balls, rolling the heavy weight of them between his fingers.

"I wish you were here," I blurt.

"Me, too." He lets out a soft sigh, twisting his wrist as he grips his cock. "I'm never leaving again."

I choke out a laugh around a moan as the vibrator hits a spot deep inside of me that no man has ever been able to reach.

He's quiet, biting his cheek as he watches me, his hazel eyes dark through the screen as he moves his hand in leisurely strokes. I'm trying to keep pace, using the wand to bring myself to the brink.

"Show me, baby," he whispers, his voice hoarse. "Show me what you like."

"I—I like—" Tipping my head back, I let out a soft groan, riding the toy and grinding against the butterfly attachment pressed to my clit.

"That's it," he murmurs, increasing his pace. "Just like that."

"I like—you—*oh*."

With a cry, I shatter into a million pieces, working the toy and strangling the silicone wand until my eyes cross. My skin is slick with sweat and sensitive, as if every single nerve ending in my body is alive and on fire at the same time.

Breathing hard, I remove the vibrator from within my pussy and turn it off, tossing it to the side.

"Johanna." Sullivan groans my name, jerking himself more roughly now, until with a strangled grunt, he erupts. I watch as he paints his chest and belly with his release. I wonder what that feels like. I wish it were my chest covered in his cum, his scent marking my skin and dripping from my breasts.

With a sigh, he sinks back against the pillows of his hotel bed. "How are you feeling?"

Taking a moment, I assess. As good as I feel, I feel the

emptiness on the other side of my bed acutely, and every mile between us feels like infinity.

"I miss you already," I admit quietly.

He exhales slowly. "I miss you, too. I'll be home before you know it."

twenty-five

. . .

Sullivan

AS MUCH AS I enjoyed the opportunities afforded to my career by attending the independent author conference, I'm much more excited to return home. Sadie and I say goodbye for now—we'll meet up back in Boston—and head to the airport. The quick hour and a half flight is painless, no turbulence. I sketch and ruminate over what's to come.

We sit on the tarmac for forty-seven minutes.

We sit on the tarmac for so long, I could freaking walk home quicker.

All in all, it takes me an extra two hours longer than anticipated to get home. I'll barely have enough time to shower and change before the party.

Maybe I can convince her to skip it.

Bounding up the stairs to our apartment, I open the door and call out, "Honey, I'm—holy shit!"

Johanna has taken the new no pants rule seriously.

She looks up from the couch, where she's painting her toenails. "Hey. You're back!" She beams at me.

I stare, transfixed. She's wearing a dark, lacy bra—from this distance, I can't tell if it's black or red—and a matching thong. With her leg up on the sofa to paint her nails, I'm afforded the beautiful view between her legs covered only by the tiniest scrap of fabric.

She frowns. "Are you okay?"

Charlotte, sitting beside her, gives a soft meow and jumps off the chair, winding her way between my legs and flicking me with her tail.

Wordlessly I shake my head. My mouth is dry, and my head pounds, all my blood rushing south.

"Is it too much?" She caps her nail polish and moves it away, folding her hands in her lap.

Closing the door, I drop my bag and approach her.

"You're never allowed to wear pants again," I tell her, before I lean down and kiss her.

Johanna lets out a soft *oomph* of surprise, her arms windmilling around before she wraps them around me, holding me to her and deepening the kiss.

She tastes sweet, like the orange soda she loves so much. The other night wasn't enough. I don't know if I'll ever be able to get enough of this.

She cards her fingers through my hair, pulling me close like she can't bear the distance between us. The soft press of her fingers on my scalp sends a shiver running through me. Goosebumps prickle my skin.

Pulling back, I stroke my thumb over her cheek. "Do we have to go?"

She laughs. "You're a groomsman, and I'm a bridesmaid."

"So?"

"So we have to go," she finishes. She looks at me, askance. "Do you really not want to go?"

I give her a soft kiss. "I know we have to. Just wish we didn't. I don't know how I'm supposed to keep my hands off you all night."

"Or... you could not," Johanna suggests.

It's my turn to look at her skeptically.

"Unless you don't want to tell anyone," she adds hurriedly. "I mean, I'd totally get it, it's fine, I won't mind—"

Silencing her with a kiss, I cup her cheek and indulge in the softness of her skin.

"I'd tell the whole world if you wanted," I whisper, leaving a quick peck on the tip of her nose. "I just don't want them to hound you with questions if you change your mind."

"I won't," she says.

My stomach churns. "You might."

"I won't," Johanna says again. She brushes my hair off my face. "You go get ready, and then we'll go to the party. Together."

"Together," I repeat, inhaling her scent. "I'm so glad we're doing this."

"Me, too," she says quietly. "I know there's a lot to talk about, but—"

"We'll figure it out," I tell her. "Just don't change your mind."

"I won't," she says again.

Charlotte jumps onto the couch, moving her furry little body between us. She nuzzles at Johanna for cuddles, flicking me in the stomach with her tail. The little wallop is surprisingly forceful.

"Okay, I'm going," I tell the cat. "Be right back."

Dropping my bag off in my room, I jump into the shower and wash the airplane stink off of me. I leave the bathroom door cracked in case Johanna needs access, but she doesn't come in.

I take extra care with my grooming, making sure to shave, trim, and shape as needed. I'm not going to assume anything will happen tonight or any other night. If it does, though... I'd like to be prepared.

I want to make this good for her in every way that I can.

She's not in the living room when I'm done. I can hear her

rummaging around in her room with soft music playing, so I know she hasn't left.

As I get dressed, I wonder what she's wearing. Should we color coordinate? Is it too soon?

Picking up my phone, I hover my thumb over my brother's contact. Do I even want to ask, or would I just be setting myself up for a decade of mockery?

With a sigh, I toss my phone back onto my bed and pull out a plain light blue shirt and a blue and green tie. Now that I'm not playing football each week and my workplace is business casual, I barely have any occasions to wear my extensive suit collection. And fuck, do I look sharp in a suit.

That just means Johanna and I will have to find excuses to dress up and go out. It's hardly a hardship to go out with the world's most beautiful woman on my arm in a fancy dress.

She's in the bathroom when I emerge from my room, doing something with her hair and a curling wand. Her face is made up now. She still looks the same as usual, just amped up to ten. Her eyes are dark, her lashes long, and her cheekbones are carved and contoured with a soft pink flush.

In the mirror, our eyes catch, and she chews the inside of her cheek.

"You look gorgeous," I tell her, approaching but staying outside of burn radius in the doorway.

"You just like that I'm naked," she says, rolling her eyes.

Letting my eyes trail down her strong back, round booty, and thick thighs, I lick my lips.

"I like you all the time." I meet her gaze in the mirror again. "I like when you don't wear pants, though."

My dick likes it, too, plumping into a solid half-chub the longer I stare at her smooth, tanned skin.

Johanna laughs, releasing the hair coiled around the curling wand and picking up a new strand. "Yeah, I'm sure."

Leaning forward, I drop a kiss to her exposed shoulder. "I'll stop distracting you and let you get ready."

Taking care of some light housework, I fill Charlotte's food and water bowls, clean the litter, and tidy up a bit. The dishwasher is ready to be run, and I could probably—

The click of high heels on the linoleum makes me look up.

And then I fall.

Head over heels, I fall.

Also—literally. I trip and fall backwards onto the couch, nearly landing on Charlotte, who gives a unhappy meow and bats at my back with her claws.

Johanna is wearing a simple red dress. It has dainty cap sleeves, a sweetheart neckline, and a soft flared skirt that falls gently to her knees.

Simple.

Elegant.

Gorgeous.

She's wearing understated black heels with a sloped wedge, making her long, muscled legs look even longer and more toned. Her hair is tied back from her face and falling in gentle waves. Her lips are painted a soft pink color matching the pink of her cheeks.

"This is a bad idea," I blurt.

Her smile falls.

"We're never leaving this apartment again," I tell her.

Johanna rolls her eyes. "You're ridiculous."

"Ridiculous about you, maybe."

With a pat to my cat's head, I straighten and adjust my tie, even though I'd much rather adjust myself in a different way. Coming to stand before her, I lift my hand to her cheek, memorizing the feel of her soft skin.

"Can I kiss you?" I murmur. My voice is husky and thick.

She bites her lip, looking up at me. Up close, I can see the shimmer on her eyelids and the light freckles her makeup doesn't quite cover.

Johanna nods.

Bending down, I kiss her softly, squeezing my eyes shut. This is what I wanted. This woman—

My hands shake, and I pull her close to hide my nerves.

What am I doing? What are *we* doing?

She lays her hand on my cheek, and I arch into her touch. "You shaved."

I nod. "I thought it was appropriate."

"I don't like it. Don't do it again." Her tone sounds serious, her eyes bright and happy.

"Noted." I kiss her again.

Johanna pulls away. "I already called a ride share. We're going to be late."

She grabs her leather motorcycle jacket and I wrestle myself into my suit jacket. She's already halfway down the stairs by the time I get the front door locked.

Down at the street, I take her hand, lacing our fingers together. She starts, then relaxes, melting into me.

"Hi," she says, ducking her head.

With a finger on her chin, I lift her head until our eyes meet.

"Hi."

"I like this," she blurts. She squeezes my hand. "This. It's..."

"I like it, too."

A dark blue sedan pulls up to the curb, and after checking the license plate, Johanna starts towards it. I open the door for her and see her eyebrows raise before she ducks into the car. Settling in beside her, as soon as my seatbelt is buckled, I immediately reach for her hand over the open middle seat, and I'm gratified when she slips her hand back into mine.

"How do you want to play this?" Johanna asks. "What are we doing?"

"What do you mean?"

"What do you want to tell them? *Do* you want to tell them?"

I shrug. "Yeah. Is there a reason we shouldn't?"

She bites her lip. "I don't know."

Squeezing her hand, I try to reassure her. "If you don't want to, we don't have to."

"There's a lot we haven't talked about yet."

"You're right. We should probably have a conversation before we spring it on other people," I rationalize.

How the hell am I supposed to keep my hands off her all night?

twenty-six

. . .

Johanna

MILES AND SAM are getting married. Yay. Wahoo.

Whatever.

I'm not a frilly, fairy-tale weddings type of person. I mean, I like reading about romance and happy ever after, but that's not realistic. It doesn't happen in real life. It doesn't work like that.

Right?

As we arrive at the rooftop bar in Dorchester, Sullivan helps me out and then immediately takes my hand, like he can't bear not to touch me for even a second.

I'm keyed up. The last forty-eight hours have been nearly unbearable. We didn't have phone sex last night, just regular conversation on video chat, but somehow, it was even more intimate than the physicality of the previous night.

But now he's back. He doesn't have any more travel planned. He's *home*.

What does that mean for us? Is there even an "us"?

Before he can open the doors to the reception, I pause, then pull him into an alcove.

"What's going on?" Sullivan asks, worry creasing his face.

"I can't do this," I tell him.

He goes still. I swear he even stops breathing.

"I can't go out there not knowing. Where do we stand? What are we?" My brain spins in a thousand directions at once. "Is there a 'we' or an 'us' or whatever?"

"Johanna…"

I start to rub my eye, then remember I'm wearing eye makeup, and curse at the crumbled mascara on my fingertips.

"I need rules. I need to know the rules." Squeezing his hand, I look up at him. "I'm good with rules."

"Okay," he says slowly. "You like me?"

Slowly, I nod. I didn't realize that was in doubt.

"And I like you," he adds. "So we like each other. And people—when they like each other, they start dating. So… we're dating?" His voice goes up into a squeak.

"And you're okay with that?"

Sullivan clears his throat. "Yes. Absolutely, yes," he says. "We're together, we're in a committed relationship, exclusive —do you want to be exclusive?"

Carefully, I nod. "Monogamy is generally my preference."

"Okay." He exhales, a happy smile on his face. "So we are dating and together in a committed, exclusive relationship. What else do we need to discuss?"

"Um…"

"I don't have a favorite side of the bed, we already live together, and we coexist fairly well in the apartment. Charlotte likes you. Is there anything else that needs to be clarified before I hire a skywriter and a billboard and tell the whole world?"

His cheeky grin makes me freeze.

"You wouldn't." My stomach turns.

"I would if I thought you wanted it," he says. Sullivan squeezes my hand. "But I know you don't, so I won't."

"To be clear, I don't want that," I tell him. "But our friends… they can know."

He pulls me close, wrapping his arms around me.

"Good," he says, before he ducks his head and kisses me.

It warms me from the inside, a pleasant flush filling me from my head to my toes. I feel wanted and appreciated, and above all else, *seen*.

He knows who I am. He's aware of my flaws and likes me in spite of them, or perhaps because of them.

There's a sound behind us, and I break the kiss but stay close to him, peeking over my shoulder.

Behind us are the two people I thought we'd have more time before having to face.

Barrett smirks at me. "Just roommates, huh?"

"Go to hell," Sullivan tells him with a cheerful smile. He wraps his arms around me, turning me within his embrace so my back rests against his front, his chin on top of my head. "None of your business."

Beside him, Diana grins. "Oh, I need to know everything."

Sullivan kisses my temple. "Maybe. We'll see."

My college teammate darts forward and grabs me in a hug. "Oh, I'm so happy for you two!"

"What's with all the hugging?" I demand. "I don't like it."

Pulling back, Diana frowns. "You don't like hugs?"

"I'm not touch averse. I just don't like hugs." As I say this, I reach for Sullivan, drawing his arm around me. "It's not claustrophobia, I'm not agoraphobic. Hugs and me just don't mix."

"I bet you like hugs from him," Barrett says, waggling his eyebrows.

I pause. "Yeah. That's different."

Diana looks sad. Hurt, maybe. "I'm sorry. I didn't know."

Sullivan squeezes my shoulder, and I take a deep breath.

"Recently… I've been doing some research, and I've found out some things that explain a lot," I announce. "I haven't been officially diagnosed, I don't know if I want to pursue that… It does make a lot of things make sense, though."

"I'm glad you're getting the answers you need," Diana

says quietly. "You know, you can talk about that stuff with me. With us. We're your friends."

"You are?" I gape at them.

Barrett laughs. "Yeah, dummy, we are. You're not getting rid of us that easily."

Bewildered, I look up at Sullivan. "They're my friends. Did you know that?"

"Yeah, baby," he says, brushing his nose against my hair. "I told you they were your friends. You don't give yourself nearly enough credit."

With a hum, I circle back around. "I didn't realize. We're friends now!" I snuggle back into the safety of his arms. "I like having friends."

"It's pretty great," Barrett agrees. He looks between me and Sullivan, his eyebrows furrowed. "Do we need to have a conversation?" he asks quietly.

"I get the picture," my new boyfriend says. "I hurt her, you'll hurt me. Got it. We're good, man." He tightens his arms around me. "I've been waiting for this for years. I'm not about to throw it away."

Diana grins at me. "Come on. Party time."

We exit the alcove and head out onto the rooftop. The party is in full swing. A bunch of people I recognize as Sullivan's football teammates are there. Most of them have brought dates.

Then again, most of them are coupled up:

There's Tucker Kingsley and Mason Prince, looking cozy near a heat lamp; Wes Bradford and Mackenzie Cavanaugh, the groom's sister, on the balcony looking out at the city below; Amir Alkatib and Deisy Cruz in line for the bar, chatting and laughing with another couple.

Greg Sawyer, the best man, is the only guy from the team to have gone pro. He's in his second year in the NFL and kicking ass. I don't think I've ever spoken to him, and I've certainly never seen him with his long hair down; it's always tied up in a bun, or in a braid on game days.

Tonight, he's sipping a dark amber liquid in a short glass, staring broodily across the party like he's competing for the surliest bastard award.

"What's his deal?" I ask Sullivan, nudging him.

"Greg is—well…" He sighs. "We'll talk to him later."

He steers me in the direction of the bar, his arm around my shoulders.

When it's our turn, he orders, "a Coke in a short glass, please."

Looking up at him, I frown. "You're not drinking?"

"I want to remember every bit of tonight." He runs his nose along the shell of my ear. "I want to be one hundred percent sober when I take you home, spread you out on my bed, and eat your pussy until you scream."

My mouth goes dry… just as another body part is suddenly, inexplicably *less* so. The moisture in my panties makes me squirm, and he breathes out a chuckle.

"Short glass?" I try to focus.

He shrugs. "This way, everyone thinks that I am, and I don't have to answer any questions about it. I'm not ashamed or embarrassed—I just don't want to address it right now."

Turning to the bartender, I order the same drink. He adds a lime wedge to the rim of the glass with a wink.

"Have a good night, y'all," he says, already focusing on the couple behind us.

Sullivan takes my hand, leading me in the direction of his friends.

My friends?

Our friends.

Deisy is smiling, Mason outright grinning.

"Look at you, man," Amir says, slapping Sullivan on the back. "You got the girl."

My boyfriend smiles widely, the scar through his lip curving his mouth into a smirk.

"Fuck, yeah, I did," he says, meeting my gaze. He winks. "What we have now was worth every single moment without her for all those years."

I wrap my arm around his waist, leaning my head on his shoulder. He smells intoxicating, with a touch of cologne or aftershave that sends my senses haywire in a good way.

He smells like home, like the soap he keeps in our shared shower and the laundry detergent we both use. He smells like his green blanket, which I've slept with every night for the last three and a half weeks.

He smells like safety and trust, like the guy who let me move into his apartment on short notice with no background check and minimal security deposit. He smells like he cares about me, like he wants to make sure I'm comfortable and safe at all times, like my happiness is his biggest concern.

But also... he smells like he did on Thursday night, spicy and fresh, nearly naked in my bed.

Tonight—

Well, I'm *prepped*. I've exfoliated and shaved and moisturized and done all the things that go along with someone hoping to get lucky tonight.

He shaved the scruffy beard from his face, too. He asked me the other night how I like to get off, and I admitted I like receiving oral the most. Did he—did he do that for me? I'm not opposed to a little beard burn... as long as it's between my legs, where I can wear it as a battle scar, and not on my neck, where everyone can see it.

Hm... I lay my hand over the side of his neck, curling my fingers around the base of his skull. He makes a curious noise but otherwise doesn't move. His pulse thuds dully beneath my palm, and I swirl my fingers through the hair at the nape of his neck.

Immediately, he lets out a soft groan, turning his head to

meet me in a sudden kiss. Sullivan plunges his hand into my hair and holds me close.

"More," he murmurs against my lips.

Dully, I hear his friends laughing, and I do my best to ignore them, focusing on the gorgeous man who turns me into putty.

His short hair whispers against my palm as I move my hand up the back of his head, and he reaches for me, moving my hand back to his neck. He squeezes, tightening my grip on his neck, and a heady bolt of lust strikes through me.

"Told you," Theo declares behind us.

I'm *really* getting tired of people barging in on us as we're kissing. Why can't they figure out that we don't want to be interrupted? Leave me the fuck alone and let me make out with my hot new boyfriend.

Josh stands tall above the crowd, rolling his eyes. "It wasn't exactly a surprise."

"Last time I saw her, she was—"

I clear my throat. "Let's not talk about that," I insert.

A few people look over in interest.

"Well, I fixed it," Josh finishes. "So now—this is expected. I knew it would happen."

"Yeah, but you didn't know it would happen *now*," his fiancé points out smugly.

"Technically," Sullivan starts, then stops when I squeeze his hand.

"Let's keep some things to ourselves, maybe?" I murmur. I don't need every single person who went to Newton to know our business.

He shakes his head. "I'm not giving him any more ammunition."

"Yeah, that's right," Theo chirps. "You tell him who's the boss, Jo."

"You can boss me around any time," Sullivan murmurs in my ear, and I shiver, squirming closer to him.

"I should have known you'd be a total Sub," his brother says, grinning.

"I'm not Submissive," he retorts.

I snort.

"I'm not. It's just that I would do anything for you, anything you asked."

Theo smirks at me. "He's totally Submissive, he just hasn't met the right Domme yet."

Amir rolls his eyes. "That's your brother."

"So? There's no shame. As long as he's consenting, I don't care what he gets up to."

Sullivan looks to me. "Yes," he says immediately.

"What?" I'm confused now.

"Yes. I'm consenting," he says. "Whatever you want, whatever I have to do—I want this. I'm consenting."

Josh scoffs, taking out his wallet and extracting a twenty-dollar bill. "I hate you both," he announces, handing his fiancé the cash. "Never thought I'd see the day Billy admitted to being a Sub."

Theo takes it with a smirk, tucking it into his pocket. "Don't worry, baby. I'll use it to buy you a new toy."

I see the exact moment realization dawns on everyone's faces, because Mackenzie and Mason both go red, and Tucker and Wes choke, and Deisy outright grins.

"This is going to be fun," she declares.

twenty-seven

. . .

Sullivan

I'M HALF-HARD ALL NIGHT. Even my brother and my friends taunting me doesn't get rid of this stiffy. The thought of Johanna bossing me around…

I let out a soft noise that any other person might call a whimper and stuff my fist into my mouth, willing my dick to behave long enough for me to take a damn leak. After nursing two Cokes all night, my bladder is protesting… and the rest of me is protesting in a different way.

At long last, I'm able to relieve myself, and after washing my hands, I go to rejoin the party.

In the dark hallway of the restaurant's alcove, hands land on my chest, shoving me roughly. Startled, I jump back, and Johanna smirks up at me.

"In there," she says, nodding towards the bathroom. "Does the door lock?"

With a nod, I let her push me into the single stall restroom, twisting the lock.

"What are you doing?" My hands fall to her waist, automatically pulling her into me. I can't get enough of her.

"You said you'd do anything for me?" Johanna strokes my chest, looking up at me.

Immediately, I nod. "What's wrong? What can I do?"

"I need you," she says, and those three words on her lips make my entire body jerk. My cock reacts immediately, swelling and tenting in my pants, and she—oh, she definitely notices, the little minx.

"You have me," I tell her, fighting my hands on her waist. "Anything you need, I'm yours."

She ghosts her lips over mine, her hand sliding up to my neck and squeezing ever so slightly. My knees buckle, and I swear she smiles against my lips.

"I need you to fuck me. Now."

Instantly, my blood runs cold. "No."

Johanna wrenches herself away. "No?"

"I won't fuck you."

"Even if I ask you to?"

"No. I can't."

"Even if I beg?"

My head spins. I feel dizzy.

"No. You don't do that." I shake my head. "You don't have to beg me to do anything."

She straightens, frowning. "But you won't fuck me."

I swallow. "I won't fuck you *here*, in a bathroom stall at a party. I want—it needs to—"

Johanna exhales. "So it's the location, not the act itself."

"If we'd been together longer than a minute, yeah, I'd go for it," I say honestly. "Our first time, though? I don't want it to be hurried and rushed in a dirty bathroom. I want to take my time."

She lets her guard down. "Okay, then can we go home?"

"They haven't cut the cake yet," I point out.

"Fuck the cake," she hisses. "I just—I need—"

Pulling her into me, I kiss her, hard. She pauses for a second before she fights back, wrestling with me for control. Yielding immediately, I give her what she wants: me.

My hands slip below the flared skirt of her dress, ruching

up the fabric in my quest to touch her soft skin. Her thighs shake when my palms land on the outside of her legs, beneath her ass. She arches into my touch, pressing her breasts into my chest.

I saw those lacy panties before—the scrap of dark red lace between her legs. My memory of a few hours ago is already fading. I need to get a refresher. Quick.

Dropping to my knees, I reach for the band of lace and edge it off her thick hips. It clings to her, the fabric damp as I work the thong down to her ankles and prevent her from escaping. The intoxicating scent of her wet cunt makes my mouth water.

Johanna's hand fists in the back of my short hair, directing my head closer to her lower half.

Well. Don't mind if I do.

Lifting the fabric of her dress, I get my first view of her pretty pink pussy, flushed and ready for me. With my eyes locked on hers, I give her a soft kiss at the top of her lips, right over her clit.

She inhales sharply, her hand tensing on the back of my head.

So I do what any person in my position would do: I dive in.

She tastes sweet like honey, her musk thick and rich. Burying my face between her legs, I lick and taste and suckle at her smooth flesh. The pressure on the back of my head increases, and I smile as I devour her, my tongue slipping through her slick folds.

They might have been teasing before, but if Johanna wants to be my Domme, I'll do whatever the fuck she wants, and I'll enjoy every damn minute of it.

My hands run over her ankles, her toned legs, her strong thighs. I pull her hips towards me and slide a finger through the seam of her legs. The heat of her wet cunt makes my balls ache, and slowly, I tease her entrance with my thumb.

She goes tense.

I stop.

And then Johanna starts to grind down on my finger, taking me inside of her.

"More," she whispers, trying to spread her legs further. The panties around her ankles keep her bound.

Shifting, I slide two fingers inside of her hot, wet pussy, and she throws her head back, pushing my face into her cunt.

I set a slow and steady pace, fucking her with my fingers as I continue to lick and suck. Drawing the bud of her clit into my mouth, I gently bite down, and her back bows. With a cry, she breaks, her walls fluttering around my fingers.

Letting her come down slowly, I wait until she releases me to stop. As I slide my fingers from her pussy, I lean back, catching her gaze. Her face is flushed, her chest rising and falling with each strained breath. Her hair is a wild mess, the curls frizzy and flat after mashing her head into the door.

She's never looked so beautiful, even when she was naked and riding my cock.

With my eyes on hers, I slowly suck my fingers clean. Johanna lets out a soft whimper.

"Fuck the cake," I tell her, my voice hoarse. I clear my throat. "I don't need ice cream or pie. I just need more of you."

"Good thing you have me," she says, panting. She squeezes her eyes shut, then exhales slowly. She's not masking—she's trying to center herself. "That was…"

"Adequate?" I grin up at her, working her panties up her legs and into place before letting her dress fall and getting to my feet. My face is slick with her scent, and I bring my hand up to wipe away the wetness on my cheeks.

She immediately tugs me forward and kisses me, no doubt tasting herself on my lips. Johanna moans, slipping her tongue into my mouth.

I like that she doesn't shy away from it. I'm not about to

suck another man's dick, but if she were gracious enough to let me come in her mouth, fuck yes I'd kiss her after.

"If that was adequate," she says, her hand curling around my neck, "I'd like to know what you actually trying is like."

After we finger-comb her hair back into place and I splash some water on my face, it's time to return to the party. We haven't even talked to the newly engaged couple yet. For two people in the bridal party, that's not ideal.

Sam is in the hallway of the alcove, wearing a white halter dress and tall heels. She has a full face of makeup and her hair is curled, which is unusual for the feisty tomboy.

"Finally," she mutters as Johanna cracks the door open.

And then she sees me.

In the bathroom.

With Johanna.

Both of us looking—*well*.

Sam's jaw drops.

"Congratulations on the engagement," Johanna says, tucking her hand into mine. "We're leaving."

Shocked, Sam nods. "Yeah. Okay."

"Congratulations," I echo, waving over my shoulder.

"Dress shopping in two weeks," Sam finally calls after us. "Be there. We're going to brunch after."

twenty-eight

. . .

Johanna

I DON'T REMEMBER the car ride. I just know that it takes too long, and all of a sudden, Sullivan and I are home. We trip up the stairs in our haste to get to our front door and it takes him three tries to get the key in the lock.

There's a soft meow when he opens the door, and we're greeted by the sight of Charlotte waiting expectantly on the other side, her furry head cocked.

"Hey, baby," he says, crouching down and picking her up. "How's my perfect girl doing?"

As the cat settles in his arms, purring loudly, she sends me a contemptuous look over his shoulder.

"Should I be worried that you call me the same pet name that you use for your cat?" I ask as I take off my coat and hang up my purse.

Sullivan laughs. "Very different connotations," he says. "She is my—well, my baby, my child."

I press my lips together, hiding my smile. "Yeah?"

"And you're…" He snags his arm around my waist, pulling me close. Charlotte's tail flicks against my ribcage. "We're a family, the three of us."

I stroke the cat's ear, and she leans into the contact, her purr increasing.

"I like that idea." Walking backwards, I pull him after me. "I just have one… well, it's not a request. I suppose you could call it a dealbreaker."

He frowns. "Yeah? What is it?"

"If we're naked," I tell him, "she's not in the bed with us. I'm not into threesomes."

Sullivan snorts. "Yeah, that's an easy one. No offense to Charlotte, but there's a different pussy I'd rather be petting."

We pause for a moment as he checks her food and water bowls, fluffs the pillow and blanket in her bed, and arranges her toys in a circle around her. The cat gives us a baleful glare and starts to lick her butt.

"I think that's a cue for us to leave her alone," he says, and I grin.

Tugging him towards my room, I close the door behind him and lock it for good measure.

Sullivan wraps his arms around me from behind, his broad chest plastered to my back. His arms are in a loose hug around me. I could break free if I wanted to.

But this embrace is entirely different from an unwelcome hugs by someone else. This—I like this. I can't explain why it doesn't bother me when other physical gestures of affection do. I just know that in his arms I feel safe and secure, and I never want that to go away.

I lift my hair off my shoulders and pull it forward. This exposes my neck, and he presses a soft kiss to the notch where it meets my spine. I shiver.

"Cold?" he murmurs, dragging his lips over my neck.

"Nope. Hot, actually."

He snickers.

"There's a zipper. Do you mind…"

His hands find the zipper at the back of the dress, slowly tugging the small tab down to the small of my back.

Most of my underwear is basic, perfunctory cotton in neutral shades that don't have visible panty lines.

Tonight? I wore my sluttiest lace bra, the one that my breasts are nearly spilling out of because it's really a size too small, and a matching lace panty set that looks hot, even if it's not the most comfortable.

There are some sacrifices that need to be made, and I'll forgo fashion comfort over curb appeal if it will make him go down on me again—and again, and again, and again.

I slip the dress from my shoulders, tugging the fabric, and then Sullivan's hands are there to help work the material over my hips until it pools around us on the floor. His fingers trace the band of my bra.

"Tell me what you like," he says. He glides his fingers up my back, tracing my skin until it erupts in soft goosebumps. He unhooks my bra, pulling it free and cupping my breasts in a gentle caress.

When I lean back into his warmth, his solid body surrounds me. His firm chest and soft belly press against me in delicious contrast, but it's the hard length pressing into the small of my back that piques my interest now.

"I like you," I say, turning to look at him over my shoulder. "I'd like you more if you were naked."

Sullivan laughs. "That can be arranged."

"I'm sure that's such a hardship for you." I press back against his erection. The solid length of it makes me shiver again, remembering it between my legs a few nights ago.

And he wasn't even naked then.

Taking a seat on the bed, I watch as he shucks his suit jacket and pulls his tie free. His neck is thick, I noticed earlier. I don't think I could get both hands around it at the same time. Inhaling sharply at the thought, I scramble back towards the pillows, pulling one onto my lap and hugging it to my chest.

"Hey." He stops, two buttons undone. "What's wrong?"

"Nothing's wrong." I blink at him. "Why do you think something's wrong?"

"You're holding onto that pillow like it's a lifeline."

I look down. I am. It's grounding me.

But I'm not anxious. I'm *anticipating*, and the expectation of the pleasure awaiting me is nearly intoxicating. Despite the fact that I'm stone-cold sober, I feel drunk and off-kilter.

I don't know how to *say* that, though.

"I'm having a lot of feelings, and they're cycling very fast," I finally tell him. "It's not bad. It's just—"

"Do you want me to stop?"

"No. Fuck, no," I say immediately. "Take it off. Take it all off."

With a chuckle, Sullivan resumes unbuttoning his dress shirt. He's wearing a simple white undershirt beneath it.

I giggle.

I can't help it.

He pauses again. "Everything okay?" he asks evenly.

"You and your t-shirts." I shake my head. "It's like my emotional support camisoles. I like wearing a shirt under a shirt."

"Yeah. It's like UnderArmor but for clothes." Sullivan shakes his head. "Do other people not do that?"

"I think it's just an athlete thing." I shrug. "I like layers."

"Me, too."

The two simple words mean so much more. He sees beneath my mask, to the me beneath the façade. He knows when I'm overwhelmed or overstimulated, and he knows when I need a distraction. He understands I have more to offer than the little glimmers I offer to the world at large.

He sees me. All of me: the good, the bad, and the ugly.

I'm not the same person I was when I started college, or even when I graduated two years ago. I'm a whole different person now, and for better or for worse, he still likes me. He still wants me.

Setting the pillow aside, I crawl towards him. I pull Sullivan towards me, wrapping my arms around his neck as I kiss him. For a guy with his sullied reputation, I thought he'd be a quick two-thrust chump, trying to lick my tonsils, but he explores me as I explore him. Even though he got around a lot in college, I still expected him to be selfish in bed.

I should have known better. I know *him* better.

His hands dig into my hips, his fingers curling into my ass cheeks, and I suddenly realize this is how *he* centers himself. Whereas I need an inanimate object with no thoughts or feelings, he needs another person to help process this.

I can do that. I can be his person.

With a sharp tug, I pull at his shirt, and he breaks the kiss to wrestle it over his head. His skin is several shades more pale than mine, dusted with dark hair. I run my fingers over his pecs and he shudders, pulling me close.

"Bad?" I ask, moving my hand to his thick neck.

"Good," he says, brushing his lips over mine. "Very good."

My fingers trail over his skin and learn the curves and valleys of his torso. A year and a half after retiring from football, he still has muscle definition in his upper body, his belly soft and rounded.

So is mine, for that matter. I lost my six-pack abs within six months after my last season ended. After a lifetime of being able to eat whatever I wanted because I was working out for a full-time job, suddenly losing that exercise source meant my body changed. I still work out, just not for thirty or more hours a week, and I'm more careful about what I eat. I've changed in the last few years, as has my body. It's not a bad thing; it's just a fact. And I'm learning to love this new version of me more and more with each passing day.

twenty-nine

. . .

Sullivan

I AM GOING to go insane. If she doesn't stop touching me—if she doesn't start *touching* me—this night might end a lot quicker than either of us was anticipating.

Pulling back, I work my belt free, then ease my pants off my hips. Johanna is there to help, pushing my boxer briefs down at the same time, making my cock spring up and slap against my lower belly.

She drinks me in, her eyes roving hungrily over my body. My hand circles around my dick, giving it a slow stroke.

I don't have a massive cock. It's something I used to be self conscious about when I was younger, especially being in a locker room setting with so many other guys with surging testosterone levels. For a guy my size, six foot three and two hundred plus pounds, I get a lot of expectations about my *size*, and I've heard a few comments from women in the past. Those typically didn't last long, as I *proved myself* in other ways…

But there's no reason to be self conscious. I can't change it or any other part of my body that makes me uncomfortably aware of myself. Nor would I. And by the same token, I would never expect a partner of mine to need to change themselves to make me like them more.

I like Johanna exactly the way she is, masked, unmasked, naked, clothed…

Although I do prefer her naked.

When I put my knee on the mattress, she scrambles away, and a part of me dies inside. She doesn't want this, doesn't want me. I'm not what she expected. I'm not what she *likes*. I've seen those toys. She likes them big.

But then—

Johanna leans back against the pillows, then works her lace thong off her hips and tosses it somewhere behind me. Her legs fall open, revealing her pretty pussy to me again.

"C'mere," she says, beckoning with her finger.

Entranced, I obey, crawling towards her. I keep my approach slow, giving her every chance to run away again. I wouldn't blame her if she did.

Johanna wraps her arms around me, pulling me down on top of her. When I try to keep my weight off her, she tugs, pulling me bodily over her. My hips meet hers, my hard cock pressed to the apex of her legs.

"Hi," she says, chewing the inside of her cheek.

"Hi." I push a lock of hair out of her eyes. "How are you?"

"Oh, you know. I'm swell," she says.

My happy smile bursts out, I can't help it.

I am seriously in love with this woman.

"How are you?" Johanna asks.

Cupping her cheek, I brush against her lips with mine. "I'm fantastic."

She twists her hips, swirling her pelvis against mine. "Good. Great. You're fantastic," she says. "Can you fuck me now?"

"As my lady commands." I kiss her gently, and when she immediately opens her mouth for me, I deepen the kiss.

My hands rove over her body, touching and memorizing.

As I slip my hand between her legs, she groans, spreading them wider and wrapping them around my waist.

She's wet, the slickness from before having increased exponentially. Her hips tip up, urging my fingers inside her silky channel. I slide in one and then a second, twisting my wrist and scissoring.

Johanna's head falls back against the pillows, thrusting her chest up.

Don't mind if I do.

Moving down the bed, I cup her breast, sucking at the rounded swell before running my tongue roughly over the nipple. Her back arches. A fresh burst of wetness coats my fingers, and I slip a third finger in, stroking steadily.

"Please," she says quietly.

"What do you need?" My eyes meet hers. With another twist of my wrist, I find the fleshy walnut-sized spot on her front wall and press on it, making her shoot upright.

"That." Her voice is strained, her breathing labored. "I need that."

Fastening my lips around her nipple again, I suckle at the bud growing taut beneath my mouth as my fingers continue to work her.

Johanna threads her hands through my hair, holding me to her, and her hand slips down to cup my neck. I have to close my eyes at the sensation as my cock jerks, and I pause to adjust myself against the mattress before continuing on with my mission.

Objective: Make her come.

So I focus on her. I give her all my attention, showing her physically how much I care for her emotionally.

And, with a cry, she breaks, my name on her lips, her back arching as a gush of wetness coats my hand.

She tugs on my hair, and as I crawl up the bed to cover her body with mine, she lets out a happy sigh.

"I like that," she murmurs, her eyes falling closed.

"Good. I like doing it." I kiss her softly. "Anytime you want, just say the word and I'll take care of you."

Johanna sighs happily. Her arms thread around my neck, holding me tightly to her, as her legs wrap around my waist. My cock presses against her pelvis, but I know she's not ready for anything more right now, so I wait patiently—as patiently as I can, given the circumstances.

"I might just have to take you up on that." Her post-orgasm voice is breathy and light.

I like this. I could get used to this.

"I hope you do."

Lazily, we make out for a bit. There's an urgency in my veins that's tempered by how blissed-out she is. I have every faith that she'll want to continue; she just needs a breather first.

And honestly, so do I. My head is spinning, my heart racing.

I've been in love with Johanna Chen since the moment we met almost seven years ago. It was—well, it wasn't love, but it was certainly lust. And as I grew to know her, it soon turned into a crush, and then deeper I fell, until I was thoroughly in love with the tightly-wound soccer player who could crush a man with seven words.

I'm not going to sleep with you.

That was the first thing she ever said to me, and though I accepted it at face value back then, I can't help but send the past version of me a thumbs up. A lot has changed in seven years. She's changed. *I've* changed. Hopefully, both of those are for the better.

I wouldn't have been mature enough to handle a real relationship when I was eighteen. Not the kind of relationship I want with her, where we have a future and a real chance at making this work. No, we'd have flamed out spectacularly, probably because of something insensitive the younger version of me said, or the snide mask she wears when she's trying to blend in.

So maybe it was a good thing she declared she wouldn't sleep with me back then. It led us to this, to now.

Her hands rove over my back, up my side, and she curls both hands around my neck. She doesn't exert any pressure, just lightly places them on my skin. It makes my heart race and my cock throb. Leaning down, I kiss her again, and she sucks my tongue into her mouth. She grinds her hips into mine, my cock trapped between us.

"I'm going to ask you something for the third time," she murmurs, fluttering her eyes open to meet mine. Her pupils are black and lust-blown, focused on me. "And depending on your answer, we'll know how this is going to go."

I wrack my brain trying to think of what she's talking about. I can't think, not with her hands on my neck like that.

"Will you please fuck me?" Johanna asks.

My smile is mile-wide. "Absolutely. Yes."

Her arm reaches out, knocking into the nightstand.

"What do you need?"

"I need you." Her breathy sigh makes me twitch. "But you need a condom."

"Got it." Slowly, I lift myself off of her, grabbing my pants off the floor. I find the condom in my wallet—brand new, put there this afternoon when I was getting ready—and return to her.

Johanna's eyes dart down to my cock, heavy against my belly, and her smile grows wide. Reaching for me, she pulls me back onto the bed, wrapping her fist around me and stroking. Her thumb presses against the leaking slit, applying pressure right where I need it most.

My groan is automatic. Her grip is tight, her strokes steady, and I can't help from thrusting into her fist.

"Later," she starts, and my heart stops. Her eyes dart around the room, looking everywhere except for me.

She's uncomfortable.

This can't end.

This can't be it.

But I'm not going to pressure her.

If she doesn't want to continue, I have to respect that. I will *always* respect that.

"Later what?"

She shakes her head, like she's trying to focus. Her eyes narrow slightly as she looks at my face. "Later, I want you in my mouth. But not now. Right now, I need you somewhere else."

Grabbing the condom, I rip it open and nudge her hand away. I roll it on and give myself a stroke, making sure everything is as it should be.

This is it.

This is happening.

Positioning myself at her entrance, I notch the tip, and her quick inhalation makes me pause.

"You okay?" I'm holding myself up, ready to pull back at any moment.

In response, Johanna thrusts her pelvis forward, taking me inside of her. She rocks against me, fucking herself on my cock.

As I slide inside of her, everything stops. My entire world zeroes in on this moment, this perfect connection between us. It's only when I'm buried balls-deep that I realize—as much as I'm inside of her physically, she's inside of me in every other respect. She has my heart. She has all of me.

And I'll give her anything and everything she could ever want or need.

Pulling back, I give her a few thrusts, getting used to the sensation. She's hot and wet and ready for me, but even though I've wanted this for *seven years*, I don't know that I was ready for it.

Johanna reaches for me, bringing our torsos in intimate

contact, chest to chest. Her breasts pressed against my pecs light a fire in my veins, and I reach down to cup her ass, adjusting the angle a bit as I pull out and thrust more steadily.

Her head falls back, exposing her neck. I taste her skin, sweet like her perfume. A soft moan falls from her lips and she tightens her embrace, holding me to her as my hips piston in and out of her.

I think back to what she said earlier. She doesn't like hugs.

But she easily seeks physical affection from me, and she takes it—she enjoys it.

Sliding out of her, I lift myself off of her and roll onto my side, taking her with me. I maneuver her onto her belly, then tilt her hips and slide back in from behind. She rolls with it, arching her back.

And then I wrap my arms around her, my forearms between her breasts and my palms against the inside of her shoulders, hugging her as I fuck her.

She whimpers.

"This okay?" I ask. Just because I think it's what she wants doesn't mean it's what she actually needs. I'm not a mind reader, and she's particularly non-verbal right now.

Johanna slides her arm beneath her, clutching at my hand. Her other arm reaches behind to grab hold of my neck, keeping me close.

My rhythm falters.

"Like this," she murmurs, arching against me. "Need this. Need *you*."

With a growl, I thrust inside of her, holding her close as I fuck into her tight, wet heat.

I need to get her there. I need her to come before I can, because that's the golden rule—her pleasure before mine, always.

Changing my rhythm, swiveling my hips, I do what I can. Her hand moves from holding mine to slide down her belly, touching herself. I can feel the tips of her fingers against my balls as she slides them against her clit, trying to bring herself relief.

It's the hand on my neck, though. She squeezes, her grip tightening on my neck, and with a shout, it hits me. Lightning flies up my spine and my cock jerks. My rhythm is erratic as I come, and I keep thrusting inside of her, trying to keep going as I empty into the condom, and she moans.

But she's not there.

Pulling out, I lift her hips, then move behind her and suck at her clit from underneath. Three fingers push into her, twisting and rubbing against that fleshy spot on her front wall.

Johanna groans, the sound deep and guttural as her walls flutter around me, clenching my fingers so tightly my spent cock jerks. Her release coats my fingers, and as I withdraw from within her, she sighs, flopping down onto the mattress.

"Okay. That's it," she says into the pillow.

I crash down beside her, wrapping my arm around her back. "What's it?"

She turns her face towards me. Her expression is sated, her eyes struggling to stay open.

"We're doing that again," she declares triumphantly.

"Now?" I choke.

"No. Not right now," Johanna says. "Just… all the time."

Scooping her into my arms, I hold her close. "That can be arranged."

thirty

. . .

Johanna

I WAKE up in Sullivan's arms. It's early, and as I glance at the clock on my dresser, I realize it's almost an hour before I usually get up. I don't generally like *sleeping* with other people, because they take up too much of the bed and hog the covers, and generally I like my space while I'm asleep.

But being in his arms? His solid body behind me, holding me close?

Yeah, I could get used to that.

There's a scratching sound, and I see a fluffy white paw stretching beneath the door.

Rolling my eyes, I pick his shirt up off the floor, slipping it on and padding over to unlock and open the door.

Charlotte bounds inside, immediately leaping onto my bed. She settles right in my spot, nuzzling against him.

Almost automatically, his hand comes up to pet her, and she nuzzles into his palm.

He freezes.

His eyes blink open.

He looks around the room. He realizes he's not in *his* room.

And then he spots me, wearing his shirt, and the sleepy

smile that spreads slowly across his face makes my heart skip a beat.

"It wasn't a dream," he says, like he can't believe it.

Shaking my head, I cross the room to him, and he pulls me into his arms.

"Not a dream," I confirm. I give him a quick kiss, nothing more than lips brushing lips. "Be right back."

Escaping to the bathroom, I take care of business and then wash my face. I didn't take off last night's makeup, and the bags under my eyes are streaked with smudged eyeliner and crumbled mascara. My hair is a wreck, sticking up everywhere and matted from sleeping with it down.

But it's the smile on my face, the lightness in my eyes, that tells me everything has changed.

I'm *happy*.

Yes, I can still feel him inside of me, his length stretching me, piercing me. My back is tight, and my muscles are sore. There's a love bite on my neck and beard burn on my chest.

It doesn't detract from how good I feel. Inside and out, in my heart and in my head, I know this is different. Last night means something. *We* mean something.

When I return to my room, Sullivan has slipped on his boxer briefs and is scratching at his chest. He smiles sleepily and cups my cheek before edging past me into the bathroom. He takes his turn, and when he emerges minty-fresh a few minutes later, he pulls me into his embrace.

"Good morning," he murmurs, kissing me.

I wind my arms around his neck, holding him close.

"I could get used to this."

His smile kisses mine. "You better."

There's a soft meow, and I look down to see Charlotte at our feet, her tail flicking around his ankle, then nudging mine with her cold little nose.

Sullivan scoops her up, puts her over his bare shoulder, and tugs me back into his arms.

"My two best girls," he says, his thumb caressing my cheek. He looks fondly at the cat. "You, you're a menace, but I love you anyway."

She starts to purr, and he laughs.

His arm slides around my shoulders, and he guides me into the main room. He deposits Charlotte on the couch, and I settle next to her, petting her furry head.

He doesn't join me, though.

Puttering barefoot into the kitchen, I watch as he turns on the coffeemaker, then checks the cat's food and water dish. Satisfied, he opens the fridge, the door hiding whatever he's doing.

Charlotte nudges me with her head, trying to get more pets, and I give her the attention she needs.

Sullivan appears before me a few minutes later, holding a cup of coffee with creamer and a plate with two toasted bagels with cream cheese. My heart thumps.

He hands me the coffee with a kiss to my cheek, then settles beside me on the sofa, his arm around my shoulders.

"What do you want to do today?" he asks. He picks up one of the bagel halves, handing me another.

I glance at my smartwatch, which I kept on overnight. "It's Monday. We have to go to work."

"We should," he agrees. "Or… we could play hooky and stay in bed."

"I like that idea." The idea of my looming project work-load makes me realize it's not a good one, though.

"How about we go out tonight?" he asks. "After work, we'll go to—"

"I like staying home with you," I interrupt.

"I do, too. We're going to do a lot of that." Sullivan grins. "But first, we need to go out on a date. A real date. There will be plenty of nights we curl up on the couch and watch a movie, or you read while I sketch, but—"

"What are you always drawing?" I've always wondered.

He leans forward, opening the drawer in the coffee table. It's not his main sketchbook, but a slightly smaller pad with plain white paper instead of the textured paper he draws on.

Flipping open the cover, I look at the first drawing.

I freeze.

It's a woman reading, and from this angle... it looks like he was sitting here in this spot, drawing while I read my book.

I turn to the next page.

It's a woman sitting at a table, pancakes on her plate. My heart thumps.

There's one of a woman wearing a motorcycle jacket and knee-high boots, holding a stack of books.

A woman with long, dark hair, holding a coffee cup, her eyes closed.

I exhale.

It's me.

He's drawing *me.*

I look at him. Sullivan is pulling at his lips with his fingers.

"I love you," he says.

My heart stops.

"I know it's soon for you, but I've been waiting for this for a very long time. I'm in love with you. And I don't expect you to say it back... I don't want you to say it if it's not true," he rushes to add. "I just... I'm putting it all out there. I don't want to hold back. Not from you, from us."

I swallow.

"I want this. I want us," Sullivan says. "I'm committed, I'm all in. Whatever you want, whatever you need—"

"I want us. I want this," I tell him. "The rest of it..." I wave my hand in the air. "I'll get there. Right now, in this moment, I'm exactly where I want to be."

He cups my cheek, kissing me, and I lean into the contact,

my hand sliding against his neck like it was made to go there. A growl rumbles through his chest, and I smile into the kiss.

A disgruntled meow breaks us apart. We both look down to see Charlotte between us, batting her paw at his knee. Obligingly, he shifts, and she jumps to the floor and stalks to her bed, glaring at us before proceeding to wash herself.

Sullivan kisses me again, distracting me from the fur baby. He holds me close, and his embrace does funny things to my heart rate.

Yeah, I could get used to this.

epilogue

. . .

Sullivan

"HERE COMES THE BRIDE" plays from my phone speaker, and my brother shoots me an annoyed glare.

"Fuck off," he mutters, shoving me. With a grin, I turn off the song.

"Boys," my mother sighs from the sofa. "Is this really the time and the place?"

My dad, standing by the fireplace, rolls his eyes. "I wouldn't expect anything else."

There are a handful of people circled around us. Sam and Miles, some of Josh's personal training clients, some of Theo's coworkers, my aunts Shana and Marie, my cousin Jessica.

And Johanna. She's wearing a gauzy pink summer dress, her long hair tied back, her makeup natural. She escorts Josh down the makeshift aisle, and I lead my brother down the same pathway. At the fireplace, we push them together, and then I take her hand and lead her to the sofa, beside my mother.

Mom squeezes Johanna's shoulder, shooting me a fond smile. We had dinner together last week and Mom has promised to send her some layman's literature. Johanna is ready to dig in and find out more, to live her truth.

Dad clears his throat. "Do I have to say the whole speech?"

"Dearly beloved, yada yada," Theo says, rolling his eyes. "Let's get to the good part."

Josh reaches for Theo. "This is the good part," he says. "Dad, please go on."

My dad gets choked up. He reaches out and sets his hand on Josh's shoulder. "It is my honor," he says thickly.

Josh's family virtually disowned him when he came out. His friends abandoned him.

He decided Theo was worth it. He decided what they had was worth fighting for.

Our family was there to catch him. He's starting calling my parents Mom and Dad, and I know it makes Theo happy; it makes me happy, too.

And as I take Johanna's hand, I run my thumb over her knuckles, imagining the ring I'll put there one day.

Not yet. We've only been officially together for three weeks. I'm certainly not ready for marriage or even proposing it.

But when I am—it will be with her. That I'm certain of.

"We're gathered here to celebrate the union of two people who were clearly made for one another," Dad says. "Theo and Josh fit together like—"

"Like birds of a feather," calls out Aunt Shana, and the assembled group laughs.

"We don't need audience participation, Aunt Shana," Theo says, rolling his eyes.

With a laugh, she flips him off, and Josh grins. He loves my loud-mouthed aunts.

"Like birds of a feather," Dad continues. "It's clear to see how much they care for one another. All I've ever wanted is for my son to be happy, and I'm so incredibly happy that he's found the love of his life, his other half. His *better* half, if I may be so bold. Because they make each other better. Theo and Josh push each other to grow, to succeed, and they're there for one another when they need a shoulder. *That* is what makes a marriage strong."

His eyes drift over to Mom, then to me on the other end of the couch. His eyes linger on my hand on Johanna's and he smiles.

"Life isn't about happy ever after. It's not about turning a page to finish the book. It's the journey you take, the path that gets you there. I hope we're all lucky enough to be on our deathbed and think—"

"Dad," Theo says, scrunching his face. "Can we not talk about death right now?"

He blinks. "Yeah. What was I saying?"

"Rings," Josh prompts.

"Right. Theo, Josh—do I have to say the next part?"

Theo sighs, scrubbing a hand over his face. "Yes. To be legal, and we *want* it to be legal, you have to."

Dad rolls his eyes. "Do you, Theodore Alexander Caldwell, take Joshua Sinclair to be your lawfully wedded husband?"

"I do," my brother says, and I swear I see tears in his eyes as Josh slips the ring onto Theo's finger.

"And do you, Joshua David Sinclair, take Theodore Caldwell to be your lawfully wedded husband?"

"I do," Josh says firmly, and Theo pushes the ring onto his finger, bringing Josh's hand to his mouth and kissing his knuckles.

"By the power vested in me by the state of Massachusetts and GetOrdained.com, I now pronounce you husband and husband." Dad waves his hand between them. "Go ahead. Kissy kissy now."

Laughing, Josh tugs Theo forward. The foot of height between them means he has to bend down to kiss his husband.

From the look of pure contentment on his face, I don't think he minds.

Johanna squeezes my hand, resting her head on my shoulder.

When Theo told me last night they were getting married, I thought he was joking. I knew they were engaged, but they just moved in together. I didn't realize they were ready for this.

Seeing our friends celebrate their engagement a few weeks ago only drove home how much they wanted it. Neither of them wanted a big celebration. They wanted simple; us, our family, a few close friends.

That's all they wanted. That's all they needed.

Aunt Marie is a professional chef, and her kitchen crew whipped up a feast for us of all of Theo and Josh's favorite foods. Jessica is a pastry chef in her mom's restaurant and made a selection of pies, as neither groom particularly wanted cake. My cousin took it a step further by making only cream or meringue-topped pies. My favorite is the chocolate cream pie with two husbands embracing.

Johanna is across the room, talking animatedly with Frank, one of Josh's clients I've met at a party. Her bright smile means she's relaxed, comfortable. She doesn't have to mask.

"You okay with that?" Sam comes to stand beside me, nodding her head at the two of them. Miles stands beside her, his arm around her waist.

"Yeah. Why wouldn't I be?" I put more snacks on the plate I'm building.

"You're not worried about him making a move on your girl?" Miles is surprised.

"Nah. Because he can make a move, but I trust her, and I trust what we have," I shrug. "If she wanted to be with someone else, she'd tell me. She wants to be with me, and I want to be with her."

He laughs. "You? It's been three weeks. I'm surprised you're still together."

"She's it. I'm in this," I tell him, snagging a glass bottle of orange soda from the cooler. "I'm all in."

Crossing the room, I join Johanna and Frank, handing her the orange soda.

She takes it with a smile and I kiss her temple, offering the plate, too. I've filled it with her favorite snacks and tasty bites, even if they're not what I prefer.

For her, I'll make sacrifices.

For her, I'll give her everything.

Johanna wraps her arm around my waist, burrowing into me. She presses a kiss to my neck and rests her head on my shoulder.

"That was nice," she says idly.

"The wedding? Yeah, it was."

"Exactly what they wanted," she adds.

"Is that what you want?" I venture carefully.

She looks up at me. "The wedding, or the marriage?"

"Yes. Both. Either."

"I don't know that I'm a big, frilly white dress kind of person," she admits. "If you wanted that…"

"I want what would make you happy." I turn to face her, holding her close. "I want you to be happy. That's all that matters."

Johanna tilts her head. "Not a big thing. My family is small, too. So maybe… we can all go to dinner, or something."

"I'll wear a tux, you'll wear a white dress with your leather motorcycle jacket." I cup her cheek, and she grins. "Just say the word, and when you're ready, I'll be there."

"You're not going to lose interest? You're not going to get bored?"

"The thought of you kept me going all those years," I tell her.

"And now? Is the thrill of the chase over?" Johanna purses her lips, looking up at me.

I shake my head. "Now, I'm thinking of *us.*"

———

Want more of Sullivan and Johanna? Read along when they explore a kink shop in this bonus epilogue.

afterword

Thank you for reading *The Thought of You*. This book is my baby and I absolutely love it to pieces.

Reviews are more important than readers realize. If you liked this book, please leave me a review!

Join my newsletter to stay in the loop! Lots of unfunny quips, unsuccessful attempts at wit, and general grouching about the writing process.

xoxo,

Allie

what's next?

Thank you for reading *The Thought of You*.

The story continues with *Sportsball is for Lovers*, featuring Sadie and the super hot guy she meets on a kink app… where she learns that six degrees of separation don't always involve Kevin Bacon…

In your hockey era? Check out *Puck Me Twice*, featuring Vanessa and the autistic hockey player she asks to be her fake boyfriend, not knowing he wants it to be real.

Want to see how it all started? Read *The Game Plan* to meet sweet cinnamon roll football player Miles and the feisty sorority girl who stole his heart.

about the author

Allie is a queer and AuDHD writer with a hyper-fixation on inclusivity and representation. She loves the color purple, Michigan football, the Detroit Lions, and the Boston Bruins. When she's not absorbed by a book, she likes to spend time with her nephews.

A San Diego, CA native now residing in South Carolina, she is allergic to the cold, rain, snow, and mosquitos.